OUR
TEACHER
IS
MISSING

Other books
by MARY FRANCIS SHURA:

Kate's House

Kate's Book

The Mystery at Wolf River

OUR
TEACHER
IS
MISSING

Mary Francis Shura

AN
APPLE
PAPERBACK

SCHOLASTIC INC.
New York Toronto London Auckland Sydney

ISBN 0-590-44597-9

Copyright © 1992 by M. F. S. Limited.
All rights reserved. Published by Scholastic Inc.
APPLE PAPERBACKS is a registered trademark of Scholastic Inc.

12 11 10 9 8 7 6 5 4 3 2 1   2 3 4 5 6 7/9

Printed in the U.S.A.   28

First Scholastic printing, August 1992

Contents

1
Miss Gretchen Dixon

Ever since I can remember, I've had this really bad habit of getting excited about new things — clothes, friends, even brand-new school years. Then it turns out that new shoes hurt, new friends change their minds about liking you, and the new teacher turns out to be just as hard to get along with as the old one. Sometimes even harder.

Every single teacher I've had since kindergarten has tried to make me over into some other kind of kid. Miss Barrett in fourth grade was the worst. She spent the whole year trying to make me "outgoing." With Ms. Wiggins in the third grade, it was "lively." Mr. Owens in the second grade wanted me louder. All he *ever* said to me was, "You're mumbling again, Eliza. Speak up!"

When school started this fall and I was assigned to the new fifth-grade teacher, I decided to use my head for once. I would keep my hopes down so I wouldn't be disappointed and cry at night until almost Christmas.

Since our principal, Mr. Heron, makes a big deal about treating us like "young ladies and gentlemen," he was waiting in class with Miss Dixon when we all came in. I only halfway listened to him saying how lucky we were to have her and that she had grown up on a ranch in Kansas and had fascinating hobbies.

I wasn't interested in all that. It was the way she looked that made my breath catch funny in my throat. I had never seen her before in my life but I *recognized* her.

Miss Gretchen Dixon didn't look outgoing or lively or given to talking in loud tones. She was even dressed in the colors I like. That first day she wore a loose gray jumper, so dark that it was almost black, with a plain white blouse and flat shoes. Her dark brown hair hung straight to her shoulders before turning up with a little flip, and her only jewelry was a watch. Miss Barrett had always worn slacks with loud sweaters, bright scarves, and chunky bracelets that clattered when she moved things around on her desk.

Even though she was a grown-up and I'm only ten, Miss Gretchen Dixon reminded me of myself. The thought that I might finally have a teacher who liked me the way I was made me shiver.

Naturally, Benjamin Hardy had to do something to make fun of her. He snickered and whispered, "Mouse," from the side of his mouth so only the other kids could hear him. Ben is into giving people nicknames, the meaner the better, the same way he is into bullying all the kids who can't or won't fight back. Even my mother, who never says anything bad about anyone because she wants to set a perfect example for me, sometimes loses her patience with Ben. "If Ben would only straighten up a little, he might be a pretty nice kid," she'd say.

I try never to have anything to do with Ben but that nickname made me mad enough to turn around and glare at him.

Even though Miss Dixon's nose was a little bit pointed and her eyes really large for such a small face, she didn't look like any rodent I'd ever seen. In fact, when she smiled, she was even pretty in a quiet way.

That was the first of September. Within that week I knew it was safe to let my hopes come up. Miss Dixon, for all her quiet ways, didn't act mousy at all. She handled our class, even Benjamin Hardy, better than anyone ever had, and she did it without ever raising her voice. By the end of the month, I was already having a wonderful time. By the week of Halloween, I *knew* that the fifth grade was going to be the best year of my whole entire life.

Then it happened.

Miss Dixon disappeared.

The weather turned cold and wet over the weekend. That Monday I overslept and started to school late. After locking my bike in the rack, I had to race to catch up with Perky Sanders who is *always* late for first period.

We were only halfway down the hall when I heard the noise spilling out from Miss Dixon's fifth-grade room. And this with the door closed. This was crazy. The tardy bell was due to ring in less than a minute unless the big clock in the front hall and my watch had both gone haywire. All of Miss Dixon's fifth-grade students, except Perky and me, Eliza Pharis, *should* already be in their seats and settled down.

Instead, I heard laughter, the thump of things being thrown against the door, and the scrape of desks being dragged across the room.

I slowed down, shifted my books to my other arm, and caught a startled breath. "Listen, Perky," I whispered. "What do you suppose is going on in there?"

Perky skidded to a stop and grinned over at me. Even before she spoke, I knew I was in for an early-morning dose of her painful humor. Perky's round blue eyes always dance when she makes what she thinks is a joke, and she pulls her shoulders up in a tight little gesture.

I like Perky, but she thinks everything she says is funny. It doesn't mean anything to her that she

4

is always the first, and usually the only person, who laughs.

"When the mouse is away, the cats will play," Perky said, giggling at her own cleverness. "Do you get it? Miss Dixon is the mouse and we're the — "

"I got it, but I don't like it," I broke in. "I'm sick of everyone making rat and mouse jokes about Miss Dixon all the time. Just because she's quiet doesn't make her a mouse."

Perky widened her eyes at me. "Honestly, Eliza, I don't know what's wrong with you lately," she said. "You used to be so easy to get along with, but this year you've gotten just plain cross."

"I'm not any kind of cross, plain or otherwise," I told her. "I just don't like all you kids picking on Miss Dixon."

"Just because you're her pet doesn't keep Miss Dixon from being mousy," Perky came right back.

I felt my face get hot. I didn't like being accused of being teacher's pet, too. So maybe Miss Dixon didn't dress in flashy clothes and yell at the kids the way some of the other teachers did, but she was fair and she was a *good* teacher. Anyway, I have always made good grades, my folks insist on it. Making good grades with Miss Dixon was easy. All she really asked was that you turn your homework in on time and not make smart remarks to disrupt the class.

"I like her," I told Perky. "She doesn't put on airs, and she doesn't yell."

"Mice don't yell, they squeak," Perky said, giggling.

I glared at her but Perky was too busy laughing at herself to notice. It's not like me to be mad all the time but every time I heard some kid use that mouse nickname, I got a little angrier.

I had tried once, right at first, to stand up for Miss Dixon against the other kids. They were surprised enough to listen because I almost never speak up. I reminded them that we were already ahead in our work and that nobody had been sent to the office yet, not even Benjamin. "Doesn't that tell you something about Miss Dixon being a super teacher?" It hadn't done any good. All it got me was a loud braying laugh from Ben.

"Listen to this, gang," he shouted to the others. "Miss Prissy Pharis is telling us we really have a Super Mouse! Wouldn't you know that the mice would stick together?"

"Lay off of Eliza," Stephen Zloty had told him. "She doesn't understand."

That startled me. I'd always thought of Stephen as a friend and here he was saying right out that I was stupid. "*What* don't I understand?" I asked.

"Come on, Eliza," Stephen said. "You haven't been paying attention. Don't you know it's not cool to act as though you like your teachers after about the second grade? It's okay to like them but not to show it."

I stared at him, something inside me pulling back from the whole idea. That was ugly, just plain ugly. "I don't care what other people do. If I like somebody I'm going to say it."

Stephen grinned at me and shrugged, but in a nice way.

The noise from the fifth-grade room hadn't let up a bit. "Miss Dixon can't possibly be in there," I decided out loud. "She's too good at keeping the room in order."

"There can't be any teacher at all in there or we would hear grown-up yelling and banging on the desk," Perky said.

"So what do we do?" I asked as the tumult grew steadily louder. "I hate to walk in on that kind of scene."

From the way Perky grinned, I already knew what she was thinking. Perky doesn't mind scenes the way I do, in fact, she sometimes starts them herself. "We have a real simple choice," she said. "We either go in and get detention with the rest of the class when the ax falls, or we hang out here and see what develops."

"But if we don't go in we'll get tardy marks," I reminded her. "I hate tardy marks." My memory isn't good enough to handle tardy marks. I hate sitting there with my parents glaring at me while

I try to remember why I didn't make it to class three months before.

Before I could decide anything, the yelling began to slack off. The laugher stopped. Almost as if by magic the hall became so quiet that I could hear the hum of voices behind the other closed doors.

"She's there," I told Perky, breathless with relief as I started for the door. "Miss Dixon was only a little late and now she's there."

"I didn't see her go in," Perky protested, racing to catch up with me.

"Neither did I," I had to admit, "but she has to be there."

When I reached the door and opened it, I expected to see Miss Dixon's slender figure behind the desk. Instead, Benjamin Hardy was standing at the front of the room. He looked blocky and solid and full of authority, holding both hands up in the air just the way Miss Dixon did when she wanted the class to be very still.

"Listen you guys," Ben was saying. "So the mouse didn't get here today. That won't be any big deal if we just handle it right. But if you keep screaming and hollering, old Heron will come charging out of the principal's office and land on our backs."

A few kids grumbled at the way he was taking charge, but he waved his hands again. "All you got to do is keep the noise down and lie low. Nobody will be the wiser and we'll get the day off. You want to take that test she threatened us with? Or would you rather just fool around and play games?"

I stared at him in disbelief. He couldn't possibly get away with that. School didn't work that way. If something came up and a teacher couldn't meet her classes, she called the office. Somebody, usually Miss Burns, the principal's secretary, covered the class until they located a substitute.

Ben saw Perky and me watching from the hall. He motioned in a bossy way and wagged his head toward the room. "Get in here and shut that door behind you," he ordered. "Quick. Don't horse around. Somebody could see you."

All I wanted to do was back away and run before this got any crazier. But Perky was behind me, giggling in that silly way and shoving me on inside.

"But what will happen when the principal finds out?" Robin Thompson asked, his voice betraying his fear.

Benjamin smiled in that sugary way that made me feel like barfing. He mimicked exactly both Mr. Heron's words and his tone. "What kind of trouble can we get into for behaving like little ladies and gentlemen until our teacher comes?"

Someone gagged softly from the back of the room which started a fresh titter of laughter. "I don't care. I don't like this," Robin grumbled, still watching the door.

"And the rest of us don't like finks who rat on us," Benjamin said, moving to where he could loom over Robin's desk and glare down at him. Robin slid lower in his seat. He didn't look up or say anything more.

I hurt inside for him. Robin is three important things: He's my next-door neighbor, my best friend, and a super all-around generic good kid.

He can't help it that he's always been slow at growing. He sometimes still gets taken for a third grader on the playground. Benjamin is just the opposite; he looks like he belongs up in junior high. Robin isn't any more of a coward than I am, and I wouldn't have stood up to Ben, either. It's bad enough that Ben is a bully but he's sneaky, too. Usually the person he picks on gets into trouble instead of him.

Stephen was waggling his eyebrows at me. I looked away quickly, knowing exactly what Stephen was telegraphing to me. Nuts to him and being cool instead of honest.

2
Enter the Troops

My stomach hurt because I was scared, but for a while most of the kids relaxed and seemed to be having a good time.

After Christopher Cobb and two other boys scuffled silently for control of the computers, they began playing games with the audio turned down. Heather and Linda wrote notes to each other and then giggled behind their hands after they read them. The kids who looked as nervous about the whole business as I was had the worst time. Some of them checked their homework while others opened library books and pretended to read. Stephen and Patrick sat at their desks with their hands folded, staring icily at Ben.

Every Monday, Miss Dixon puts fresh flowers in the glass bud vase on her desk. When she goes to her parents' ranch in Kansas over the weekend, she brings back sunflowers and black-eyed Susans. When she stays here in the Chicago suburbs where we live, she brings local plants. The wild

11

asters from the week before had collapsed into a circle of dry leaves and pollen dust around the bottom of the vase. There was something pitiful about those dead flowers because I knew Miss Dixon would have put in new ones, if she had been here.

I decided to look up the only unanswered question on the October Bulletin Board Quiz.

All my teachers before Miss Dixon had assigned kids to decorate the bulletin boards. The students generally took their themes from the holidays and used a lot of things put out by greeting card companies. Since school had just started, none of the kids said anything when Miss Dixon decorated the September board with pictures she had taken and developed herself. She had tied this photo display in with science.

September had been "Wild Flowers of Autumn," with wonderful color photos of white Queen Anne's lace and blue chicory along with a lot of other flowers that I had to look up, even though I realized I'd seen them all my life. Miss Dixon had put a number under every flower. Kids who identified all the flowers correctly and turned the list in on the last day of the month got their names under a star on the board. I really like independent projects like that, so I made myself a promise. I was going to get my name under a star every month that Miss Dixon held a contest.

When Miss Dixon put up the October board with

the title "Birds of Our Area," a lot of the kids grumbled.

"October is Halloween," Linda told Miss Dixon. "Every other room will have bulletin boards with bats, black cats, and jack-o-lanterns."

"Yeah," Ben said. "And really good gross stuff like Dracula with blood on his teeth, and deadly scorpions, and big, nasty, poisonous spiders."

"You kids can decorate the windows any way you want to," Miss Dixon had said genially. "I get to do the bulletin boards. I'm a teacher, remember? And I just happen to know that you can't look at an exhibit for a month without *something* soaking into your brains."

"But I like Frankenstein better than I do dumb old birds," Dan said.

Miss Dixon smiled at him and touched the Nikon camera she kept on the corner of her desk. "I'll make a deal with you, Dan. If I see a dumb old Frankenstein flying around our forest preserves, I promise to take his picture just for you."

Realizing they had lost the first round, the kids tried to negotiate for November. "Well," Ben said, as if he were doing Miss Dixon a favor by giving in, "just so we get to do turkeys and pilgrims next month."

Miss Dixon laughed softly. "Come on, who are you kidding? You know you're sick of the same old Thanksgiving pictures. Would you believe you're going to get leaves for November?"

When the whole class groaned, she only smiled. "One thing I can say about you fifth graders, you *are* predictable."

I liked looking at all the pictures in the bird exhibit except the blown-up photograph at the top. A giant crow was perched in an oak tree above the clutter of a rundown farmyard. With its beak wide open and its broad black wings spread, it looked as big as an eagle and twice as mean. This was the kind of bird that bad dreams are made of.

I took the field guide off the reference shelf to look for the small brown bird with the sharp beak that I still hadn't figured out. It was so tiny next to the twig beside it that I wondered how Miss Dixon had caught its picture at all, much less such a clear one.

"Telescopic lens," Miss Dixon had explained. "They do wonders at catching the tiniest detail."

I kept turning the pages of the guide, but Ben's crazy business got in between my eyes and the pictures, making the birds all look alike.

If only I had never let Perky push me into the room! Worst of all, I couldn't imagine how this was going to end. I can't stand it when I can't figure out the ends of things.

I sneaked careful glances around the room. I wasn't the only one getting more and more nervous as the hands of the clock crawled toward the end of the first hour. A lot of the kids wriggled in their seats and looked around at each other almost desperately.

When Stephen rose and started walking toward the door, Benjamin moved quickly to block him. He stood with his back against it, glaring at Stephen.

"Where do you think you are going?" he asked.

Stephen stopped walking but he didn't back down. "How about the bathroom?" he asked. "Or should I raise my hand and ask for permission?"

Benjamin scowled at the laughter in the room. "I know you, Stephen Zloty. Old hero chicken. That bathroom bit is a big lie. You mean to go straight to the office and tattle. That's what comes of your being a cop's kid, a sense of *duty*." He pronounced the word as if it were something really gross.

Stephen said, "This was an okay game for a while, but it's not now. Nobody wants to get in trouble, especially with a Halloween party coming up. We could all get detentions because of you."

Some of the kids piped up in agreement but Benjamin just sneered at Stephen.

"Besides," Stephen went on, "did you ever think that something could really be wrong with Miss Dixon? What if she had an accident or something, driving from Kansas clear back here to Illinois? Nobody is going to know she needs help unless they know she didn't get here."

15

"So there would be one less mouse in the world. Who really cares?"

I wanted to shout, "I care!" but didn't dare to do it.

To my astonishment, a low angry murmur began at the back of the room. "A joke's a joke," Patrick Warner called to Ben. "Yours quit being funny about twenty minutes ago."

"Don't tell me you give a hoot what happens to the mouse," Ben said with a sneer. "Or maybe you've turned chicken, too?"

"Never mind who I'm worried about," Patrick said. "Let Stephen out to go to the office."

Benjamin kept his back pressed against the door, gripping the knob to keep anybody from grabbing it.

"Anyone who leaves this room has to go through me first," he said, glaring around at the guys who had gotten up one by one to come and stand behind Stephen.

Looking past Ben, I saw someone pass the door, then stop and come back. I let my breath out with relief as a face peered through the glass window in the door.

The art teacher, Ms. Worth, her hair pulled back above giant, dangling gold earrings, was staring into the room and frowning.

Stephen saw her, too. "Jig's up, Ben," he said quietly. "Look behind you."

16

"Yeah, sure, chicken," Ben said, sneering at him. "That's only the world's oldest trick."

It was weird to watch Ben's face change. His skin even looked pale and rubbery as he felt the doorknob begin to twist in his hand. When he turned to see who had hold of it, Ms. Worth jerked the door open.

She came in swiftly, making the whole crowd of boys back off. "All right, clowns," she said, her eyes flicking over the room and back to Benjamin and Stephen. "What's going on here? Where's Miss Dixon?"

"She didn't come," Benjamin said swiftly. "I was just going down to report it to the principal."

Ms. Worth looked astonished, then laughed right in his face. "I've had you in class, Benjamin Hardy. Do you really expect me to swallow that?"

"We were just behaving like little ladies — " Benjamin began.

Ms. Worth rolled her eyes up as if she were helpless, which I was sure she never has been for one moment of her entire life. "Spare me the angel act, Ben," she pleaded.

Then she frowned thoughtfully. "Come on, class. Are you telling me that Miss Dixon never showed up at all? She didn't come in and then have to take a call or something?"

When the kids all shook their heads or sang out

"no," she turned to me. "Eliza," she said. "Do me a favor and run down to the office — "

"Oh, please, not me," I wailed, knowing I would never be able to explain that last hour to the principal or anyone else.

Ms. Worth shook her head. "All I want you to do is take a message. Just tell Mr. Heron that I'd like to see him in Miss Dixon's fifth-grade room as soon as he can get here."

I didn't exactly drag my feet going down the hall but I didn't run, either. I told myself I didn't *have* to run. In fact, I wasn't *allowed* to run. Running in the halls was strictly forbidden even if I had wanted to get to Mr. Heron's office in a hurry, which I didn't.

I am into fairness because I believe in it even though no one else seems to. Is it fair for teachers to criticize a kid because she's not outgoing, then give her hard errands to do because they know she won't stand up and fight to get out of doing them?

Mr. Heron was in his glass-walled office talking on the phone. I swallowed hard before giving the message to his secretary, Miss Burns. Until that minute I hadn't realized that I was more afraid of Miss Burns than I was of the principal himself. She looks a lot like the masks that hang on each side of the stage in the auditorium. Her eyes and mouth look alive but her face never bends anywhere.

"What's this all about?" she asked me.

I only shook my head and repeated Ms. Worth's request word-for-word.

"As soon as he can get there?" the secretary repeated as if she were giving me another chance that I didn't deserve. When I only nodded, Miss Burns gave up and scribbled a note with lots of the words underlined. After glaring at me, she took it into the office and placed it in front of the principal.

He read it and looked out at me before he finished his conversation. The minute he replaced the phone, he strode out into the reception room. "What's up?" he asked me.

I repeated Ms. Worth's message again without changing a word because she said that was all I had to do. Mr. Heron looked at me steadily for a minute, as if he could see right through my hair into my brains. "All right," he said, his voice rising a little. "If that's how you want it."

His legs were so long that I had to skip now and then to keep up with him going down the hall. When we passed a boy from kindergarten coming out of the washroom, the little kid pressed himself against the wall. His eyes were dark marbles as he stared after us.

Smart, I decided. There was a kid who had learned Stephen's system early on. Right outside the fifth-grade room door, Mr. Heron looked down at me. "Now let's see if we can solve Eliza's mystery." I wanted to tell him that it wasn't my mystery at all, but he already had the door open and was striding in.

Except for Christopher Cobb, who lives in his very own world of silicone chips and intergalactic travel, everybody watched the principal's face as he talked quietly with Ms. Worth. No one smiled, not even Ben Hardy.

I wished Mr. Heron hadn't used the word *mystery* and that Stephen hadn't asked such scary questions. I couldn't stand to think about Miss Dixon having an accident, so I didn't. I just took my seat and listened, too.

3
Theories

Mr. Heron's secretary filled in until a substitute teacher could be found. Miss Burns didn't pretend she liked being there. Apparently, she didn't intend for the class to like it very much, either. She walked straight into the room without even looking at us. She sat down behind Miss Dixon's desk, emptied the bud vase into the wastebasket, and brushed the dead flowers and pollen onto a piece of paper and threw them away, too. She frowned as she shuffled through the papers piled on the right side of the desk, then looked over her glasses at us.

"I have before me a list of your assignments for today," she said. Her mouth was turned down like the mask for tragedy. "In spite of your efforts to the contrary, I intend to conduct this class just the way your normal teacher would have done."

"But, Ma'am," Benjamin said, smiling in that sticky sweet way. "We don't have a *normal* teacher. We have Miss Dixon."

The ripple of laughter and foot scraping that swept the back of the room was silenced instantly when Miss Burns looked up at him. She stared at Ben a moment, then flipped the attendance record open on the desk. "Hardy, isn't it?" she asked, holding the book open with one finger.

When he nodded, she scrawled a mark in the book. "Unfortunately for you, Benjamin, I have a good memory for behavior as well as for names. I'm sure we'll all do better without your smart mouth in here. You may take your books with you and go to the office. Mr. Heron told me he would be prepared to deal with anyone who acted up in this class."

Ben stared at her in disbelief.

She stared right back.

When he finally caught his breath and opened his mouth to argue, she broke in, twisting her wrist to peer at her watch. "I think I made myself clear. Now close your mouth, take your books, and go to the office. I might add that you'll get one extra demerit for every thirty seconds you delay in leaving this room."

I have never seen Ben Hardy move that fast before.

A hard knot developed in my stomach as the morning wore on. By noon, it was shoving itself up to fill my whole chest. Miss Burns had given us the test that Ben was trying to avoid. She had moved on swiftly to the next assignment, making it sound as if it would take a week to do.

I couldn't believe she would open a class discussion so close to the lunch bell. Class discussions are danger times two. The teacher might call on me and I wouldn't know the answer. The teacher might call on me and I *would* know the answer but couldn't squeeze a sensible sound past a sudden tight place that grows in my throat when my name is said aloud in class.

When the lunch bell finally rang, the class filed out of the room quietly. They were still talking only in whispers when they got down to the lunchroom.

Robin caught up with me. "Did you have the feeling that we should have saluted going out?" he asked me.

I grinned at him, not daring to try talking yet.

"At least any substitute teacher we get will look good after that," Patrick said. "And with Ben gone, maybe nobody will give her a hard time."

"I don't want a substitute teacher," Robin said in a bleak tone. "I think we should complain. Teachers aren't supposed to disappear without warning like that."

"Oh come on, Robin," Patrick said. "Not coming to school isn't the same as disappearing. You know Miss Dixon must have some good reason for not making it today."

Perky gave me that dancing-eyed look. "I have a theory," she said.

Patrick looked daggers at her. "If you say the cat got her, I'll hit you."

I looked at him and smiled a little. Patrick could be a little dense at times but for once he was thinking for himself. I was glad to hear that somebody else was as annoyed with Ben's mouse business as I was.

Perky's face fell and she looked cross at having her joke spoiled. "You said it, I didn't," she reminded him.

The hot lunch was listed as wieners with baked beans, my least favorite. The hot dog had split open and drained out its juice to make a dank marshy place on the bun. Something square and bleached-looking stuck up from among the pale pink beans whose sauce was making the bottom of the bun as soggy and gross as the top.

Patrick picked up his hot dog, wiped it on his napkin, and ate it with his fingers while he stared off into space.

"What kind of reason do you think Miss Dixon could have for not coming?" I asked him.

He shrugged. "I wouldn't blame her if she couldn't face one more day of Ben Hardy, but I doubt that's it."

I had to swallow my milk fast to keep from giggling and spilling it all over myself.

"The chances are very good that she's been kidnapped," Robin suggested. "Kidnapping is big these days. Kidnapping, holding people hostage, and making airplanes fly where they didn't intend to go."

"Miss Dixon wouldn't be in any airplane unless she went on some really big trip. When she goes to visit in Kansas, she drives her car," Stephen told him, sounding more than a little disgusted. "She lives in one of those big houses on the other side of the public library."

"How come you know so much about her?" Robin asked.

"Sometimes I ride around in the patrol car with my dad," Stephen told him. "I've seen her go in and out of the back door carrying in groceries from her car. It's gray."

"Mouse gray," Perky put in. I refused even to look at her, and she was the only one who laughed.

"Hey, Robin," Patrick said. "If you want to make up a really wild scenario, how's this? She's secretly married to a mobster. Maybe her husband finds out they have put out a contract on him. He decides to squeal to the cops to save his neck and the FBI whisks Miss Dixon off. They put her in one of those witness protection programs with a new name and social security number and everything."

"And new clothes," Perky put in, getting excited over the whole idea. "That would be wonderful! No more of those dark jumpers in every color known to corduroy. They'd dress her in black leather pants and miniskirts and give her a punk hairdo. Even her own mother wouldn't know her."

Stephen had apparently given up on anyone making sense. He didn't even respond to this new silliness but went on eating his sandwich moodily, staring at his plate.

When Christopher leaned across the table, I looked up in surprise. Chris is strange, but who am I to talk? Chris parts his pale hair in the middle and lets it grow almost as long as a girl's. He seems to be happy living in a world all his own. I've never known him to listen to anything but the strange voices inside his own head since I have known him. I certainly had *never* seen him pay the least attention to anything that was said at the lunch table. This time he had clearly been listening enough to come up with a theory of his own.

He peered out from between strands of hair with a serious frown. "You didn't happen to see her carrying groceries this weekend, did you, Stephen?"

"Well, no," Stephen said.

Chris nodded. "Has anyone seen her since school let out Friday?"

"None of us were looking," Stephen said, sounding a little exasperated.

"The timing can be significant," Chris told him. "If she's been missing for two and a half, almost three days, she could be in serious trouble. We mustn't discount the possibility of an alien force intercepting her sometime over the weekend. With that much time to work in, they could have used their advanced technology to surround her and imprison her in a zone of invisibility. Once that was done, they had plenty of time to whisk her off to their home planet."

"But why?" Patrick asked. "Why would they want the mouse?"

I kicked him under the table. He knew how I felt about people calling her that! He scowled at me and rubbed his leg as Chris went on.

"If I were selecting a model individual to instruct my planetary populace in the peculiarities of the inhabitants of the planet Earth, Miss Dixon would be my primary choice," Chris said.

I stared at him with astonishment. Did that mean that Christopher Cobb *liked* Miss Dixon or that he thought she was peculiar?

"You'd choose Miss Mouse?" Perky squealed in surprise.

"Lay off," Robin grumbled. "It's rude to squeak ill of the absent. Chris just means that she's pretty decent as hominids go."

"Quit interrupting Chris," Patrick said, staring at him dreamily. "Come on, Chris. Give us more details about this kidnap force. And that zone of invisibility — is it like those two-way mirrors? Would Miss Dixon be able to see out through it?"

Patrick admits that he hardly ever understands what Chris is saying but that doesn't keep him from hanging on Chris's every word. "It's like having some great science fiction writer right here among us," he said. "If I could spell those words he uses, I'd record them for history."

Stephen stirred restlessly in his seat. "Come on, guys, get real!" he said. "Miss Dixon has not been hijacked in any airplane. She is not married to any gangster. She has not been whisked away by alien forces. She's a regular sort of person who prowls around on her bike taking pictures with that camera of hers.

"If anything *has* happened to her, it's something ordinary. Bikers have accidents. People get thrown off bikes. Maybe she's wandering around with amnesia not remembering who she is."

"At least that would keep her safe from the aliens," Christopher said, nodding. "What they would really want to extract from her would be her body of knowledge about civilization on this planet."

"Stop that with the outer space!" Stephen said, raising his voice with anger. "If Miss Dixon hasn't had an accident, if she *has* been whisked away, she has been taken for some logical earthly reason. Maybe she saw a crime committed and the criminal is holding her captive until he gets away with the loot."

The bell rang and I followed Stephen over to

dump my untouched lunch into the garbage can. He made the most sense of all. The kids are always talking about Stephen's father being a policeman. I'd never seen Mr. Zloty dressed in a police uniform, driving a car with a bubble on top, or pulling anyone over for a traffic ticket. I did remember seeing him in a regular suit on TV, being interviewed about different kinds of crimes — things like bank robbery and the man who stole a lot of money with his computer.

"We don't have a crime wave or anything going on right now, do we?" I asked Stephen as we went out into the hall.

He stopped so fast that I almost ran into him. "What made you ask me that?" he asked, looking at me with his eyes narrowed a little.

I stared at him and then grinned. "Maybe I was paying too much attention to all that crazy stuff."

He relaxed a little and grinned back at me. "Forget all that silliness. You surprised me by asking about a crime wave. My dad has been so busy the last couple of months that at home he's practically a missing person himself."

4
Mouse Games

Although Benjamin returned to the room as soon as class started, he only sat sullenly staring at his desk. He didn't even try his usual game of "bait the substitute." That was just as well because the woman who came to replace Miss Burns had shiny dark eyes that darted around the room as if she were afraid of missing something.

Actually, I wondered if it wasn't us kids she was afraid of. She had obviously been recruited at the last minute with no warning at all. She had a kind of shattered look, as if she couldn't really believe what had happened to her afternoon.

She seemed to have dressed in the dark with no mirror, and her hair was glued into place with so much hair spray that every time she moved, the air smelled like varnish.

There were four syllables in her last name. She wrote it on the board and made the class repeat it out loud three separate times until we got it right. Then she began to work her way through the afternoon schedule.

I couldn't believe how well-behaved everyone was. Neither could I believe how stupid we all sounded! She droned on and on, reading from the book because she didn't know any more about history then we did. Just when I knew for sure that the fuse in the electric clock had blown and it would be two-thirty for the rest of my life, Mr. Heron came in.

When he looked toward the row where Benjamin Hardy sat, Benjamin shrunk about an inch in all directions.

Mr. Heron effusively thanked the substitute for "seeing us over a tough spot." Somehow the kids managed not to laugh when he pronounced her name wrong before excusing her for the day.

I sighed inside when he came around and sat on the front of Miss Dixon's desk with his hands crossed loosely on one knee. I hadn't been through four years at his school without learning that this was the way he sat when he had come to talk us kids into something.

None of these had been things we *wanted* to do. I remembered riding on the Harvest Parade float under big banners asking everyone to vote for the new school bond issue. You could hardly hear our parents clap for the booing of the taxpayers who didn't have kids in our schools.

31

"I know we were all surprised and disappointed when Miss Dixon didn't report for work this morning," he began. "I thought it would be quite simple to locate her once we realized she wasn't here on the school premises."

He paused and looked sternly at Ben again.

I fought a crazy impulse to giggle. A few more glances like that and Ben would shrink so small that even Robin and I could manage him.

"Now I realize that I was optimistic. As you know, Miss Dixon came new to our system just last month, in September. Since she has taken advantage of the nice fall weather to make several trips back home to Kansas to visit her family, none of us has had the opportunity to get to know her well. This has made it harder for us to contact her."

"You mean she's still lost?" Patrick asked.

Mr. Heron didn't appreciate his directness. "We're not using the word *lost*," he said with some irritation. "We are sure there's a logical reason for her absence. We are continuing to make every effort to contact her. Since we haven't been able to reach her by phone, we have assumed she might have gone home to Kansas this weekend. It's possible that she is on her way back here right now, and we will hear from her any minute. But that's all aside from what I came to say."

"Is this the first teacher you've ever had disappear?" Christopher asked in a tone of scientific curiosity.

"We're not using the word *disappear*, either," Mr. Heron said, his voice sharp with frustration. "Sometimes it's inconvenient or even impossible to contact people by phone when one is traveling. Believe me, Chris, both our administrative staff and the police are working very hard on trying to locate her."

I almost felt sorry for Mr. Heron. Principals and teachers never forgot for a minute that kids are sent to school to learn. But they hardly ever remember that we learn more stuff *outside* books than we ever do from inside them. The kids stirred in their seats the way they always do when they have decided someone is trying to put something over on them.

"Can I ask what word we *are* using?" Stephen asked.

"No," Mr. Heron said curtly. He was sorry at once, but really had no place to go from there. "What I mean, Stephen, is that all this talk about what word we are using is not what I came in to discuss with you." He tried to smile. He was better-looking when he didn't try to smile without meaning it.

"In our attempts to locate Miss Dixon we have asked the police in Kansas, Missouri, and our own Illinois State Patrol to be on the lookout for her car. Unfortunately," he went on swiftly, "this, along with our other inquiries, has triggered the interest of the media. I am afraid that something may be said on this evening's news about Miss Dixon being missing. I am just alerting you to this fact because we don't want you or your parents to be unduly concerned about Miss Dixon. Of course we are all very intent on locating her, but we're *sure* there is a reasonable explanation for her absence. We have *every* confidence that we'll find it right away."

I had never heard that room so quiet. The kids sat staring back at Mr. Heron in complete silence. Mr. Heron glanced at us only a minute before looking away. He seemed to be the only person in the room breathing. I felt my own breath come short.

I know he thought he was keeping us from worrying about Miss Dixon, but he had managed to do just the opposite. By telling us he didn't even know enough about why she hadn't come to school to put a word on it, he had made me, for one, what he would call unduly concerned.

He stood up with his chest out a little, as if to convince us that he was in complete control. Then he looked around brightly and rubbed his hands together.

"Thank you for your attention and for behaving like young ladies and gentlemen. Now if you will rise by rows, you may be excused before the final bell."

"Word games," Patrick grumbled as we got our coats out of our lockers. "If they still haven't found her, then she's lost."

"Or kidnapped," Robin suggested again. He glanced at me. "Coming, Eliza?"

"In a minute," I told him. I really wanted to ask Stephen if Mr. Heron had made him worry, too.

"I'll see you at home then," Robin said, starting off down the hall with his jacket only half on.

"Or disappeared," Perky was saying as I turned back to the other kids. "I wonder how long they wait before they put those pictures on milk cartons?" I wanted to hit her. If she thought *that* was funny, she was sick.

"I'm going straight home and contact the other members of my skywatch group," Christopher said in a brisk businesslike way. "Maybe someone saw a mysterious craft land or saw a blip of one on a radar screen."

I stared after Chris as he followed the others out of the front door. Only Stephen and I were left.

Stephen laughed softly. "Eliza? Do you think that between us we may have cornered the fifth-grade market on sanity?"

"I guess I'm pleased that they even care," I told

him. "I've had about all the mouse games I can stand."

"From the way they went after Heron, you would think Miss Dixon was everyone's favorite person. But nobody ever had a good word for her until she disappeared." He glanced over at me. "Except you, Eliza, that is. It takes guts for a fifth grader to run up the flag for a teacher."

"Not for me," I told him. "I like her. She's a lot the same as I am."

"How do you figure that?" he asked, his voice rising with surprise. "You've got long legs and she's kind of short. Your hair is that red silky color and your nose is more like a button than a pencil point."

I swallowed and decided to let the button nose pass. "I don't mean we *look* alike. I mean we're the same kind of people." My words spilled out without my even thinking. I heard myself saying things I had never even thought before. But they felt so true that I stumbled on.

"She's not 'outgoing' the way Miss Barrett tried to make me. She's not forceful the way my dad thinks I should be. She only talks when she has something to say, but that's different from being shy, which Mom says I am, too. She likes to do quiet things like read and draw and take pictures with that camera of hers. She isn't the least bit loud or violent, but that doesn't mean that she doesn't know what she believes in. And she always tries to do what she should."

The minute my words were out, I felt myself shrink up inside. Had I made both of us sound dull and stupid and mousy? I didn't care. Miss Dixon and I were the way we were, and we both had a perfect right to be that way, even if people wanted to call us names. I glared at Stephen, daring him to laugh at me.

He didn't laugh. Instead, he just looked at me steadily for a long minute. I've always thought Stephen had a nice smile but his face is also nice when he isn't smiling, and his eyes stay very steady when he's thinking. Finally, he nodded as if he had worked something out inside his own head. "You may have hit it on the nose, Eliza. But quit glaring at me! There's nothing wrong with any of that. If you two are so much alike, you ought to have some idea why she didn't turn up today."

I shook my head. "I haven't made up any wild theories like the other kids have. I only know for absolute sure and certain that Miss Dixon knew where she was supposed to be. She would have come if she could or she would have contacted Mr. Heron no matter how inconvenient it was. That's the part that puzzles me. It even scares me a little that some bad thing might have happened to her."

"Eliza, I don't mean this to be insulting, but I

have to ask you something and you have to promise not to get mad. Now be honest with me, don't you spend a lot of time being scared about something or other?"

I *knew* my face was scarlet. "Maybe I do," I admitted.

"And don't you think it's silly to make such a big deal about her only being gone one day?"

"Well, maybe," I conceded. "But you were the one who said she could have had an accident or something."

"She'll probably turn up before they even run the evening news. And if I find out anything through my dad, I'll call you tonight."

"I'd like that," I told him.

He looked around. "Where's Robin?" he asked.

When I told him that Robin had gone on home, he laughed. "Are you sure he knows the way home without biking there with you?"

"He's my best friend," I reminded him.

He nodded. "I know that." Then he smiled. "Come on. You don't live too far out of my way for me to bike you home. Just in case you don't know the way there by yourself."

5
Only One Day

Mom works at the public library. We usually get home about the same time unless she gets delayed or goes shopping. That day, Stephen and I beat her home. We found Robin sitting on the front steps with his arm around my dog Simon. Stephen stared at Simon and whistled. "Wow, has that fellow ever grown since I saw him last! What is he anyway?"

"A dog, what do you think?" Robin sounded insulted.

Stephen laughed and gingerly held out his hand. "I can *see* that he's a dog. It's just that I thought he was a Lab but he's so much bigger than most Labs are."

Simon sniffed Stephen's hand, then sloshed it all over with his big pink tongue. "Nice fellow," Stephen said, nodding to Robin.

"He's Eliza's dog, not mine," Robin said. "I have a fish." Robin looked up at me. "Your mom came home from work and then went to the grocery store. I reminded her that she was out of peanut butter sandwiches."

"Robin finished them," I explained to Stephen. "He's crazy about graham cracker sandwiches with chunky peanut butter in between."

"And he eats them at your house?"

"He has a little trouble telling our kitchen from his."

"Oh, no, I don't," Robin said, shaking his head. "Yours is the one with the good things to eat in it."

Stephen looked confused, but I never know how to explain that Robin spends almost all his time at our house. It makes good sense because Robin's family has so many kids and my folks have only me, which isn't nearly enough. Robin started coming over every day when he was about three. He just never quit coming. We even take him on family vacations with us because, otherwise, Mom keeps looking for him and worrying. It's nice, like having a brother.

Stephen shrugged. "I wouldn't mind living next door to a well-stocked kitchen myself," he admitted. He stood, rocking his bike back and forth. As he spoke, my mother turned into the drive with the deck of her station wagon filled with grocery bags. Simon leaped off the stairs and loped across the lawn, barking a welcome. Stephen stood up straight on his bike. "I've got to shove. Remember to watch the news and I'll call you later."

After Robin and I pushed Simon aside and carried the grocery bags inside, Mom opened a box of ice cream bars and handed one to each of us. Simon got his treat on the back porch because he's as sloppy as he is oversized.

Then Mom smiled at me. "How was your day, Sweetie?" The "Sweetie" made me go all soft from feeling sorry for myself.

"Awful," I said, not even bothering to pretend.

Mom, who had been sorting groceries, stopped and looked over at me. "That's not like you, Eliza," she said. "What's wrong?" Then she leaned over to lay her face against mine. She smelled of hand lotion and the plastic seat covers in the car. That comfortable smell only made me swallow hard.

"It was so awful that I can't bear to talk about it," I told her.

She pulled out a chair with her free hand. She sat down and drew me tight against her. "Okay, Robin," she said, looking over my head at him. "You tell."

"From the beginning?" he asked bleakly.

"From the beginning," she said, not sounding terribly happy.

"First off, our teacher disappeared."

"Disappeared?" Mom asked with a little squeak in her voice. "What does that mean?"

"That's just one way of putting it. She didn't come to class today. But I'll never get through

41

telling this if you keep interrupting," Robin complained.

She nodded and sighed. "Fair enough. First Miss Dixon disappeared, then what?"

"Ben Hardy wouldn't let anyone out of the room to report it to Mr. Heron."

"That Ben Hardy!" Mom said with exasperation. "I'm sorry, Robin, go on."

"Ms. Worth came in and Eliza went to get Mr. Heron and we had Miss Burns until noon and after that a substitute teacher who smelled like paint."

When he stopped, it was so quiet that I could hear the kitchen clock ticking. Mom waited a minute more before she spoke. "So basically, Miss Dixon didn't show up for classes, and you all had a bad day. That doesn't sound really awful to me."

When Mom turned away, I watched her with astonishment. How could she listen to Robin describe that awful day and really have her mind on the groceries the whole time? But right away she went back to sorting things in swift jerky movements — the frozen things into the freezer, fresh vegetables into the sink, and cereal boxes and crackers and paper goods all out on the table, to be stacked in the pantry.

I wanted to cry. What kind of a mother could be so interested in cheese and butter and bags of carrots when her only child in the world had gone through the worst day of her life?

"You don't understand," I told her. "It's awful

having just a substitute. We had Miss Burns *and* a substitute, too! And I don't care how hard Mr. Heron says they are trying to find Miss Dixon, I don't think he has any idea where she is. They are even going to talk about it tonight on the TV news."

Mom turned to look at me thoughtfully. "What makes you think they will?" she asked.

"Because Mr. Heron told us they might and that we were not to be unduly concerned."

She hesitated another minute, then nodded. "That sounds sensible enough to me. I suggest we wait for the news before we go completely to pieces. Is that a deal? In the meantime, you kids must have homework, even if it was only assigned by a substitute teacher who smells like paint."

I let the TV run without sound while Robin and I did our homework. When the news actually started, I turned it up. Mom came in wiping her hands on a towel. She stood in the doorway clear through the local news.

The anchorman talked about the newest events first: suspected arson, and an argument in the city council that almost brought two aldermen to blows. Then he did an update on the break-in and theft at a local chemical plant that he had reported on the week before. He explained that the missing potassium chlorate was potentially extremely dangerous if it fell into the wrong hands. That although the chemical was used in the manufacture of ordinary household necessities like tooth-paste and mouthwash, it was also used to make fireworks and explosives.

Mom was looking really restless by the time they went on to the national news, then the sports and the weather, with double ads in between each of them. She was about to give up and go back to the kitchen when the local newscaster came back on. He was smiling in that smart-aleck way Perky smiles when she thinks she is going to say something funny.

"In closing," he said, "we have a variation of the man-bites-dog story for you tonight. Instead of a student playing hooky, Miss Gretchen Dixon, fifth-grade teacher at Roosevelt School, failed to show up for classes today. Mr. Gregory Heron, Principal at Roosevelt, did just what he would have with an absent student, he called her home.

"When he was able to reach only her recording machine, he appealed to our version of Scotland Yard (the local police) to assist him in his role as Sherlock Holmes. Since Miss Dixon often spends her weekends in her native state of Kansas, the school authorities have also contacted the state highway police in the states she would have traveled through on her return to the Chicago area.

"Mr. Heron's diligence was finally rewarded. After repeated attempts to reach Gretchen Dixon's parents in Kansas, he learned that the family was attending a relative's funeral in Wyoming.

44

Case solved. Mr. Heron hopes to have word from Miss Dixon before school convenes tomorrow."

They didn't even show a picture of Miss Dixon, but only Mr. Heron smiling into a microphone out in front of the school.

"Why would anyone go off to a funeral in Wyoming?" Robin asked in a confused way.

"Because people die there, too," Mom said in a dry quiet tone. "Robin, you scat on home now. Eliza has to wash up for supper."

Mom didn't even mention Miss Dixon at dinner. She only told me to finish my meal so she could start the dishes. "One of Dad's out-of-town clients is in town," she explained. "Dad promised we would spend the evening with him. You know the rules, Eliza?"

Dad owns an insurance agency and keeps really strange hours. When he and Mom started letting me stay home at night alone, they gave me rules. Mom doesn't have just a few rules. She has something like a complete manual on "How to Behave When You Are Alone in the House." I knew the whole thing by heart but she recited it over to me again anyway. Then she dressed up, checked the locks for the third time, and left to meet Dad for the evening.

She hadn't been gone very long when Stephen called. "I hope you didn't swallow the stuff that clown was handing out on the news," he said, sounding really disgusted.

"He made me sick," I told him.

"This is the real scoop and there's nothing mysterious about it. Nobody has made any real progress toward locating Miss Dixon. They've been calling her phone number all day but keep getting her voice on her machine asking that the caller leave a message."

"What about the family all being at that funeral out in Wyoming?" I asked.

"Just hearsay," he said. "They never actually reached Miss Dixon's parents in Kansas. When they kept calling and calling, some neighbor woman finally broke in on the party line and told them that was where her mother and father had gone. Nobody knows whether Miss Dixon is with them or not."

"Maybe she never went to Kansas," I suggested. "Did anyone check her house?"

"I leaned on Dad a little," he admitted. "He told me the local police had checked at her address here in town. It's that house I've seen her go into with her groceries. Since nobody was home, the police checked with the neighbors. They learned that Miss Dixon has a little apartment on the top floor and watches over the house when the owner is away on trips."

"Surely her landlady knows where she is?"

"Dad says they're trying to follow up on that, too. But no luck yet," he said. "The landlady is visiting her grandchildren down in Phoenix. Now they're trying to find the woman's forwarding address in hopes that she knows something."

"It sounds like the police just rang the bell or something," I told him. "Couldn't the police go into that house and see if she's there?"

"No way. When I suggested that, Dad got all red and started yelling at me. He asked me if he didn't have enough on his hands without a bunch of kids nagging at him about nothing."

"Nothing!" I said. "It's something to us to have a missing teacher."

"He made a good point, Eliza. Miss Dixon has been missing only one day. Those chemicals from the plant have been gone over the whole weekend. Finding them could be a life-or-death matter. Terrorists could blow up planes with them, or use them for sabotaging military places, or even blow their way into banks."

Maybe that one day just seemed long to me because I like Miss Dixon so much. Before I could say anything, Stephen went on. I could hear the laughter in his voice. "While Dad was ranting, he told me what else is going on in town. Somebody is climbing into backyards and shaving the hair off pedigreed English sheepdogs, and a peeping Tom is sending people into hysterics in the subdivision west of town."

I didn't feel like laughing. "After all," he went on, "it's only one day. We just have to wait and see what the authorities can turn up."

47

"That's not good enough," I said. "You know where that house is. We could go look around there for ourselves."

"You mean tonight?" he asked, his voice squeaking a little. "What would your folks say?"

"They're out for the evening," I told him. "It wouldn't take long. Maybe Miss Dixon's back by now and I can quit wondering. Maybe she got sick in there or hurt so that she couldn't reach the phone. Maybe we wouldn't learn anything at all, but the least we can do is go and look around."

Stephen was silent.

"Look, if you're afraid, just give me the address and I'll do it alone."

He groaned. "All right, Eliza. But if we get picked up for prowling, I'm the one who'll get his head taken off. Look for me. I should make it over on my bike in about ten minutes."

Before I could even thank him, he clicked the phone. He had sounded half mad, but if my folks found out I had left the house without permission, they would be mad *all the way*!

Forever.

6
Strange Lights

Stephen pulled up on his bike exactly ten minutes later. For a dumb dog, Simon has a lot of intuition. Because he *knew* I wasn't supposed to creep off in the dark with Stephen, he started barking the minute I went out to get my own bike. I couldn't leave him making all that racket or Robin's mother would eventually come over to see if everything was all right. I went back inside and put half the leftovers from our dinner into his dish. I hoped Mom would just think I got hungry before I went to bed. It was bad enough to be a sneak without having to make up a lot of fibs, too.

And it was *dark*!

Low heavy clouds had buried all the stars. Now and then the moon managed to slip between the clouds long enough to cast a sullen greenish glow for a minute or two. That was all the light we had except for street lamps. They weren't much help, glowing weakly through the damp mist trailing along the streets. Stephen's frown was as dark as the night. He set off pedaling silently through side streets to avoid running into any cruising police cars.

Miss Dixon's apartment was in one of the old houses, set back from the street behind a deep lawn thick with huge maple and oak trees.

"There are lights on," I told Stephen as we walked our bikes up under the shadows of the trees.

"That probably doesn't mean anything," he said. "People put their lights on timers when they go away on trips."

The closer we got, the spookier the big old house seemed. Stephen had said that Miss Dixon had a little apartment on the top floor. As tall as the house was, it had only three floors, with what looked like a pretty small attic with dormer windows above that.

When we went up on the porch, I realized that the light I had seen was on the main floor where the living room would be. When I pressed my face against the window, I saw the light spilling out into the hall from a room whose drapes were drawn.

Stephen kept glancing toward the street as if he were afraid we would be seen. When we couldn't see anything from the porch, we went on around in back. The garage was locked, but by staring through a clouded window for a long time, we made out a car parked in one stall, with the other one empty. The bike rack along the opposite wall was empty, too.

"That might not mean anything, either," Stephen said. "People who really like to bike always have those racks on top of their cars. Miss Dixon could have taken her bike back to Kansas with her."

Stephen was making me angry, always saying things might not mean anything. No matter how many things he explained away, the house still seemed spooky to me. When I backed up against the garage to stare at the upper windows of the house, I saw something even Stephen couldn't explain.

"Up there," I said, pointing. "That dim green light coming through the square window on the second story of the house. Don't tell me *that's* not spooky."

He narrowed his eyes to stare at it, then grinned at me. "I give you spooky on that. I haven't any idea what it can be."

"It looks as if it is coming from somewhere in the hall at the top of the stairs," I decided. "Maybe she fell down the steps into that hall, and that's a flashlight she's trying to signal with."

"It's not moving back and forth," he said.

"She could be too weak to move it by now," I suggested.

He stared at me. "Where do you *get* those ideas?" he asked.

"Because I'm worried, that's all," I snapped at him. "Nothing would make me happier than to have Miss Dixon turn up at school tomorrow, but that won't make it any easier until then. I think one day is a lot longer than your father does. I'm going to try to get inside."

He groaned and slapped his head. "*That* you do alone, Eliza Pharis," he said, sounding mad again. "Prowling is one thing. Breaking and entering is another."

"Maybe I won't have to break anything," I told him. I couldn't possibly feel that spooky about the house without something being wrong in there. "Anyway, somebody has to stay outside and be a lookout."

I didn't even wait for his arguments. I started around the house trying to figure out how to get inside. The only way I can get into our house without a key is through our basement windows. Mom opens them when she's doing laundry and then forgets to lock them when she's through. She doesn't worry because they are too small and narrow for anyone but a skinny kid to get through anyway.

These windows were like ours, hung from the top. The first three I tried were locked tight. One was even covered with something dark on the inside. The hook on the fourth one was poised above the ring and hadn't been pushed all the way in. Stephen squatted to watch me try to jiggle it loose.

"You don't really want to go in there anyway," he said.

"You don't *want* me to," I told him. "That's different." Just as I spoke, the hook slid off to the side so I could push the window in.

I backed in, so I would land on my feet. All the time I was worming my way through that narrow slot, Stephen kept protesting. I knew he had finally given up when I let go to drop myself to the floor. "Don't leave your fingerprints on anything," he whispered through the open window.

Dark, darker, darkest.

Even if I had a flashlight, I would have been afraid to use it much. I had landed in the laundry room which was neater than ours at home. I almost cried out when I saw the peanut butter jar with matches in it sitting beside the gas water heater. At least I could make a tiny bit of light in a real pinch. I took a handful of the matches because the jar wouldn't fit into my jacket pocket.

Outside the laundry room, the basement was nothing like ours. A huge furnace and air-conditioning unit filled one wall. I was just turning away when something breathed behind me, then made a grating sound. For a minute I was too scared to move. Then a blower went on and I realized that the thermostat must have signaled the furnace to go on. I was still alone in the basement. Beyond the furnace was a wall of storage on tall metal shelves and then a door with a huge sign on it.

DO NOT OPEN THIS DOOR, it read in giant letters.

I stared at it a moment remembering those stories about villains with locked rooms in their castles and what awful things happened to the people who *always* looked behind those doors before the story was over. I tried the door anyway. I was safe. The doorknob wouldn't turn in my hand and there wasn't a sign of a key anywhere.

I had to feel my way everywhere I went, but at the top of the basement stairs, it was easier to see. Some light filtered in from the outside and lamplight glowed along the polished floor of the hall.

I tiptoed through the rooms as if someone were listening. In the kitchen, the refrigerator was empty except for about six kinds of mustard, half-filled bottles of pickles, and some unopened cans of tomato juice. The living room, where the lamp was lit, was filled with furniture draped with sheets like Halloween ghosts.

I wanted to be out of there, out with Stephen, back across town and in my own bed. But I had come too far to leave without finding out about that strange green light.

The green glow became more intense at the turn

of the stairs. When I heard the soft bubbling noise, I almost laughed out loud as I ran the rest of the way up the steps. A huge aquarium took up almost all the space between two doors. The fish were tropical, brightly colored with wonderful, graceful fins. The bubbling of the air into the tank stirred the delicate green fingers of water plants, and a huge snail oozed along the glass inside.

Remembering Stephen's warning about fingerprints, I covered my hand with the tail of my shirt as I opened the first door I came to. Right away I knew this had to be the landlady's bedroom. A giant four-poster bed was flanked with tables piled high with books. Another long table was covered with framed pictures of young, modern-looking people. The wall behind it reminded me of my grandmother's bedroom. Women in corsets and men with long beards (some wearing ridiculous hats) stared back at me from big gilt frames. My grandmother's pictures like that are all of relatives that she says are "long dead and gone." A bathroom door stood open and the air smelled faintly of lilacs.

I passed another door without opening it and went on up the stairs where Miss Dixon's apartment should be. That hall had only two doors. Just as I got there, I heard a telephone ring behind one of the doors. I stood listening to it and shaking all over. After the fourth ring I heard Miss Dixon's quiet level voice come on the machine, and I began shivering even more. It was spooky to hear her voice sound so natural when I knew nobody was there.

I opened the wrong door first and saw a narrow flight of stairs going up into the attic.

Opening the second door almost sent me staggering backward into the hall. The air smelled so bad that I didn't want to breathe it.

In that awful moment I remembered hearing terrible things about how dead people smelled. I don't know whether I was crying, but my eyes watered as I went in and raised the shade to get some light into the room. The room was neat, with one of those sofas that becomes a bed and some nature photographs hanging on the walls. This had to be Miss Dixon's apartment, but I didn't see anything that could cause that dreadful sickening smell.

Beyond this room was a tiny kitchen where I really couldn't breathe. The table was set with a pale blue place mat, and dead asters hung over the side of a blue vase. The smell was coming from a clear covered dish, where ground meat had been set out to defrost.

I turned and ran back downstairs.

I had been right to worry about Miss Dixon, even if she had only been missing one day. People don't set meat out to defrost unless they intend to come back right away and use it. Something had happened to keep her from coming back and fixing her supper. But what?

I was halfway down the stairs before I remembered the fish and wondered how long it would take them to starve to death. I had to fight to keep from crying about that. Robin has a wonderful fish named Grendel. I know we would both cry if Grendel ever started floating on his side the way dead fish do.

Stephen was jumping up and down out there. He peppered me with whispered reproaches while I struggled to pull myself up on the sill to get back through the window. Finally I just yelled at him, "Shut up and help!"

He caught my wrists to try to pull me up. I had just gripped the sill with both hands when he let go of my wrists and whispered, "Drop!" in a scared tone.

I hit the floor in a heap, hardly breathing.

From down there, I saw a light play against the side of the garage and through the trees. After it passed, Stephen was back at the window. "Hurry up," he whispered. "Quick, give me your hands."

I was trembling so hard all over that I didn't help him much at all. When he finally pulled me through the window, I just collapsed on the cold ground. I kept rubbing my wrists and bawling, not even able to explain what I was crying about.

"How long does it take hamburger to rot?" I asked.

He stared at me a minute then pulled me to my feet.

"Listen," he said. "The police just went by here on their residential patrol. We were lucky they didn't see me there at that window. Quit this with the rotten hamburger and let's get out of here."

It felt good to breathe clean air again.

The fog got heavier as we cycled toward home. We were several blocks from the house when he slowed down and pedaled his bike alongside mine. "Okay, Eliza," he said. "What happened? What did you see?"

I told him about the locked room in the basement and the fish tank and why Miss Dixon's kitchen smelled.

He didn't say very much at all but I knew he wasn't mad this time, only thinking. "At least we know she didn't plan on being gone," he said when we got to my house. "But that doesn't necessarily mean that she's still around here someplace. Maybe she was called away and forgot about the hamburger. Eliza, it's still only one day."

"At least we know she isn't in that house, lying hurt somewhere," I told him.

He shook his head. "Boy, you sure are stubborn."

"What harm does it do for me to look for her? I have as much right to do it as Mr. Heron does."

"If she's really missing, and I'm not saying that she is, then it's police business," he said. "My dad is dead set against amateurs fooling around in police business."

"So how can you call this police business when he admits he's not doing anything at all?"

He chuckled. "Good point, Eliza. I tell you what I could do. I could call the other kids and ask them to try to think of places Miss Dixon might have gone to. Tomorrow at lunch we could pool everything we know and see what we come up with. We'll have to be careful," he added. "We don't want everybody in school to find out what we're doing."

"Why not?" I asked.

"I told you already! Dad warned me that if I poked around playing amateur detective, he would see to it that I ate standing up for a week, that's why not."

7
The Abnormals

The rain woke me up when it started in the night. I burrowed into my pillow trying to forget how scared I had been in that house. I told myself that if I went back to sleep, the rain would stop and Miss Dixon would be at her desk by the time Robin and I got to school.

Wishing doesn't make things come true.

I must have turned off my alarm the first time I woke up. Suddenly it was light, and Mom was shaking me and I barely had time to get dressed and swallow some cereal before Robin was at the door.

He was all bundled up in rain gear, which made Mom send me back for my own. Robin catches colds easier than I do. He catches colds easier than anybody, and never lets them go. His nose gets snuffly when the first flake of snow falls and he coughs clear through spring.

He was squeaking with excitement. "Boy,

wasn't the news something this morning? Are we ever getting coverage at Roosevelt School!"

I stared at him. This had to be the one school day in my entire life that I didn't make it to breakfast in time to see the news. "They found Miss Dixon?" I asked quickly.

He shook his head. "No, but the fact that she's missing was one of the big stories. They told about her not coming to school yesterday and about how nobody had been able to locate her yet. They even showed a picture of her, camera and all. They asked anyone with any knowledge of her whereabouts to get in touch with the police or the school administration."

I didn't say anything because I couldn't. I kept smelling that hamburger she had set out but never cooked.

"The worst of it is that we'll have a substitute again today," Robin went on.

"The worst of it is that she's missing," I told him, glaring so fiercely that his eyes got all round. I almost never get cross enough at Robin to bark at him like that, and I was sorry the next minute. I told him so, and he nodded that it was all right. But he didn't say anything else all the way to school.

The halls were louder than usual with everyone talking about Miss Dixon and wondering where she could be and what had happened to her. I started feeling scared again — the way I had in that dark house the night before.

The rain really got serious after we got to school. It swept down in such dark waves that the substitute teacher had to turn on all the lights. Even then the room felt dismal and enclosed. The construction-paper bats and witches that the kids had hung in the windows glued themselves to the sweating panes and dripped orange and black tears down the glass.

The substitute had just finished marking the attendance book when Mr. Heron came in. He told us he was sorry not to have news of Miss Dixon but that we were not to worry, everything possible was being done to find her. When he closed by asking us to come to him with any information we could give, Stephen caught my eye. That was silly of him. I wasn't about to tell anyone about going into that house and seeing that hamburger.

This new substitute didn't smell like paint but she was relentlessly bubbly. Maybe she was only trying to raise our spirits but her high voice kept rocketing up and down like an elevator until I wanted to scream. *I had been right all the time. Miss Dixon would have come if she could. Something was terribly wrong if the police and everyone else couldn't find her. I wouldn't let my mind think the word* dead *but it kept spelling itself in my brain anyway.*

When the lunch bell finally rang, I was the first one out into the hall. "Look who's hungry," Stephen said, catching up with me.

I shook my head. "I just can't wait to see if any of the kids has a good idea of where she could be."

Stephen frowned. "Even if somebody has a good idea, we can't go looking for Miss Dixon in this pouring-down rain."

"Lying in a ditch with a broken bicycle on top of you for maybe two whole days is a whole lot worse than getting a little wet from rain," I told him.

"Brother," he groaned, looking at me as if I were some other person. Then he went ahead of me into the lunch line as if he didn't like that new person very much.

The hot lunch was pizza. The cheese had risen in rounded bubbles, which had burned black from being left in the oven too long. I poked holes in my cheese bubbles until the rest of the kids brought their lunches over and filled up the table. Perky looked over at me and then looked away again as if she didn't *want* to recognize me. Stephen had looked at me as if I was a stranger, too. Maybe I really was!

Nobody even mentioned that Miss Dixon was still missing or suggested that we try to help find her. Instead, they started to talk about the new substitute and to make their lame jokes. Nobody had a good word to say about her, and Perky tried to imitate the way her voice went trilling up and down.

Why had I ever thought I liked these kids? They were nothing, really nothing. All they could do was sit and say smart things to show off for each other. Even if they couldn't *like* Miss Dixon, she was a human being. Couldn't they tell that something was awfully wrong when even the police and the principal and the TV station had become concerned?

Whatever was simmering down inside my chest threatened to boil over. More than anything I wanted to wake up the others, get them to care so we could find our teacher.

My anger must have changed my face because Stephen leaned toward me. "What's the matter, Eliza? You feel sick?"

I glared at him. "Maybe I'm not myself anymore. But you're the ones that are making me sick. We know Miss Dixon better than anyone and what are we doing to help find her?"

"What do you expect us to do?" Patrick asked. "Be detectives ourselves? Like the street kids in the Sherlock Holmes stories — the Baker Street Abnormals?"

"They weren't Abnormals, they were Irregulars," Chris corrected him. "Actually an Abnormal is more like a mutant."

"Stop that!" I yelled, jumping to my feet. "You're nothing but a bunch of sit-down comics."

I started to stamp off but Stephen caught my arm and held me back.

"Come on," he coaxed. "Losing it isn't going to help. Sit down." I glared at him, and I didn't let him pull me back down into the chair. Then he turned to the others. "All right, guys," he said seriously. "Sure, Eliza is acting pretty freaked-out, but she's also right. The police wouldn't show Miss Dixon's picture around if they weren't concerned, too. Have any of you thought of anything that might help them find her?"

"I thought a lot after you called last night," Chris said. "But I didn't turn up anything helpful. I did get a report from one of my associates in Skywatch, though, about an apparent phenomenon late Saturday night." Chris stopped and stared thoughtfully at his pizza crust.

Patrick leaned forward breathlessly. "Around here somewhere?" he asked.

Chris shook his head. "At first he thought it was over Bangkok."

I groaned and tried to sit down, but Stephen was in my way.

"On closer examination it turned out to be a smudge of peanut butter on his telescope," Chris went on. "One of the guys suggested I contact the space program at NASA to inquire if they had received reports of UFOs."

"Wow!" Patrick breathed. "What did NASA say?"

Chris shook his head. "We decided that they wouldn't tell us the truth anyway because of security restrictions." Then he looked over at me. "I did write down all the data I had accumulated about Miss Dixon." He pulled a printed sheet from his pocket and handed it to me.

"Data," Patrick repeated, obviously impressed. "All I know is that she has a gray car and I only know that because Stephen told us."

I should have known what would be on Chris's list. He had written down the kind of camera and film Miss Dixon had and what computer languages she knew. Anyway, he had tried. "Thank you, Chris, for trying," I told him.

"She probably went some place where there are lots of leaves," Perky said. "Remember, she warned us that instead of turkeys, she was taking pictures of leaves for the November bulletin board?"

"But November will start Saturday," Patrick said. "She can't get pictures back in time to have them up on Monday."

"She develops them herself," I told him. "She has her own darkroom and everything." I almost added that her darkroom was in her basement but stopped myself in time. Until that moment I hadn't realized what the locked room with the black cloth over the windows was for. Not that it helped.

"Listen, Eliza," Stephen said, suddenly sounding excited, "I just had a great idea. Perky's right. Miss Dixon did say she was going to take leaf pictures for the bulletin board. The oldest trees around here are over by the mill on York Road. You know how dangerous that millpond is. It's so dark and overgrown that its banks are always slick with moss."

I saw the mill in my mind as he spoke, slimy banks along a deep green pool crowded with mallard ducks and Canada geese. The trees were huge, shading the water where the giant mill wheel turned to run the grinder.

"We could bike over there right after school and look around for any sign of her," Stephen went on.

"Someone hires a man to watch over that place," Patrick said. "Wouldn't he have noticed if she'd drowned in that pond?"

"Drowned people usually sink and don't come back up for about three days," Chris said.

I wanted to kick them both hard but what was the use?

"All I've ever seen that old man do is let tourists in and out of the mill and yell at kids for not putting their bikes in the lot across the road," Chris went on. "I can't imagine him really looking for anything that might go wrong."

"I'll go out there with you," Robin offered. "I said I'd bring Mom some stamps. I'll drop them at home and meet you."

"I have to check in at home first, too," Patrick

said. "But I could bike out there to meet you afterward."

By the time we had decided to meet a half hour after school was out, the bell signaled the end of lunch hour. I stared down at the hollow craters of burned cheese on my pizza and pitched the whole thing as I walked out of the lunchroom.

I didn't know whether to feel good or scared about what we were going to do. I couldn't think of anything good that could happen to Miss Dixon out at the mill, but at least we were trying.

The other kids ran ahead, but Stephen and I left the school together. I was buried in my thoughts. As we passed the corner of the building, Ben Hardy jumped out at us from nowhere. He was smiling broadly as he shouted.

"Guess what, guys! They found her! They found her!"

I stopped and stared at him. A wild sort of excitement rose up in my chest. I was so happy that I practically yelled at him. "Where is she? Is she all right?"

I hadn't noticed that Ben was holding one hand behind his back. He pulled the dead mouse out and swung it by its tail right in my face. It was a small mouse with its paws curled delicately over its chest and its back feet pointing down like a ballerina's.

"Right here!" he shouted. "She was trapped!"

Maybe I screamed. I didn't remember later.

But then I didn't remember swinging at him, either. I'd never hit anyone in the face before in the entire ten years of my life. I was startled at how much it hurt my hand. I probably wouldn't have been able to knock Ben down except that he didn't expect it. But neither did I.

He sat back on the wet playground, bracing himself with one hand and rubbing at his mouth as he stared up at me.

All the fury that had prompted me to hit him was gone. I stared back at him dumbly.

His baseball cap had fallen off, leaving his hair as messy as a Halloween fright wig. His broad face was pale except for the redness starting to show where I had struck him. Mingled blood and spit trickled from the corner of his open mouth. I scrubbed my fist hard against my jeans, shuddering a little because my hand felt so nasty from hitting his open mouth and wet teeth.

Then he must have seen himself the way I saw him. He roared like a monster on TV and scrambled to his feet to come after me. His face was already beginning to darken and swell a little as he struggled up. I was still frozen there when he lunged at me with both fists swinging.

Stephen was too quick for him. He caught Ben's arms from the back, yelling at him to lay off. Didn't he know what Mr. Heron would do to him for hitting a girl after what he had already done? Ben stared at me, his eyes red with hate. I swallowed hard because my throat felt tight.

"You're lucky, Pharis," he mumbled angrily. "*This* time you're lucky."

Stephen handed him his cap, then stood there waiting. Ben walked a few steps with his chest sticking out, then darted behind the side of the building where he had come from.

Stephen grinned at me. "You told me you were fed up with the mouse games. I guess I believe you now."

I nodded, not wanting to speak for fear I might cry.

"Hey," he said. "Don't look so downcast. If Miss Dixon is as spunky as you are, she's going to be okay."

I was still in a daze when we reached the mill where the kids were waiting. "Hey, Robin," Stephen called. "I bet you think you really know Eliza."

Robin glanced at me. "Nobody knows her any better than I do," he said with satisfaction.

"And she couldn't surprise you?"

I felt myself turning red as Robin glanced over at me again. He shook his head. "Not a chance."

"I'll give you three guesses what she did after the rest of you left school this afternoon," Stephen said, avoiding my glare.

"Do you have to tell *everybody*?" I asked.

He nodded soberly. "Everybody in the whole town, Eliza. The more people who know what you did, the less chance that Ben will try to get even."

"That doesn't make any sense to me," I said crossly.

"Come on," he said. "Think about it. You know what a sneak Ben is. He only does things he thinks he can get away with. If enough people hear what you did to him, he knows he'll be suspected if anything happens to you."

I wailed without wanting or meaning to and covered my face with my hands. "Enough mystery already!" Robin said as the other kids crowded around. "What could *you* do to Ben?"

"She hit Ben in the mouth and knocked him flat on his backside, that's what," Stephen said. "That sock she gave him was a beauty. What I wouldn't give to have *that* on videotape."

"I don't believe it," Robin whispered, staring at me. Patrick and Chris stared at me, too, with open mouths.

"Believe!" Stephen said. "We may be seeing the dawn of the New Age of Eliza."

Even at that hour traffic was heavy along York Road. We left our bikes in the parking lot across the road, then had to wait forever to get across it again.

First we searched all around the stream for bicycle tracks. Since Miss Dixon was new in town, she might not know that it was practically a federal offense not to park in the lot. We gave up on that hunt and looked instead for signs that someone had walked along the bank, lost his or her balance, and fallen in.

It was impossible to search those bushes along the banks of Salt Creek without getting drenched. Stephen and Patrick went along the north side, and the rest of us took the south. We reached the deep millpond at about the same time. You could see only an inch into that dark green water.

"Oh for a wet suit!" Stephen said, kneeling to peer into the pond.

Perky called out, "Do wet jeans and a sweater count?"

For once I laughed at her joke before she did.

"Maybe we can find a big branch," I suggested. "Then we could poke around down there and see if it snags on anything."

Patrick and Robin found one. They had dragged it clear across the road and almost down to the pond when an angry man's voice yelled at us, "You there, you kids!"

Stephen stood up and dropped his end of the limb. "That's the man who works here," he groaned. "I thought he'd be off home by now."

The man came right up and glared at us. There was nothing to do but stand and listen to him yell. He *acted* as if the mill belonged to him; he *looked* as if he had been there the whole century and more.

He didn't have to tell us the place was a historical landmark. We already knew. Who would have hired him to take care of just any old mill? He didn't have to tell us how many people had drowned, or nearly drowned, there in the last hundred years, either. Our parents always warned us with those stories whenever we visited there. It was only when he told us to get that big branch out of the pond before he called the cops that we really listened to his lecture.

Robin and I took off for home at top speed. I couldn't pedal fast enough to outrun my awful consciousness that night was falling on the second whole day that Miss Dixon had been a missing person.

8
The Third Day

Things started to go wrong first thing that Wednesday morning. I had to hold my toothbrush in my left hand because my right hand hurt so much from hitting Benjamin Hardy.

Hitting Benjamin Hardy!

I had waked up so worried about Miss Dixon that I had forgotten about knocking Benjamin down. I stared at myself in the bathroom mirror with the foam all around my mouth like a mad dog, and fought back tears. Mom and Dad didn't know about that fight but they would. Sooner or later they hear about everything. I knew how mad they would be and what a long talking-to I'd get. I'd be in college before they'd let me forget about it.

Hot painful tears spilled out of my eyes even though I scrubbed hard at them with my pajama sleeve. Why did I have to be an only child anyway? None of my friends were. Other parents learned that they couldn't get perfection in one single kid and gave up expecting to. They didn't try to *talk* their kids into goodness the way my folks did me.

Perky's parents sent her to her room with no stereo or TV. Stephen's father swatted him on the backside. Even Robin's mother didn't try to "talk" to him. She yelled at him so loud that I could hear her clear from next door. I know I try harder than any of them to be a good kid and then I get "talked" to with words that sting my mind and can't ever be forgotten.

I must have stood there longer than I meant to because I heard Mom call, and went on getting dressed. Hitting Ben Hardy had happened. Sooner or later I would have to pay for it. But right then, I needed to get downstairs to see the morning news.

Dad usually only looks at the top half of the news over the rim of his newspaper. That morning he put the paper all the way down to watch and then looked over at me.

"Is this your Miss Dixon they're talking about on the news?" he asked.

I nodded because I didn't want to cry into my cereal.

Mom must have given him one of those warning looks because he changed his attitude. "Well, it's pretty exciting to have your school featured on the news, isn't it? You *know* there's a perfectly reasonable explanation for why she hasn't been in touch."

"No, I don't," I said, because I didn't know that.

He looked a little surprised and then got huffy, the way he does when anything upsets Mom or me. "The police and TV people are irresponsible to raise such a fuss and upset these young people. Someone should speak to the mayor."

Then he rose and touched my cheek with his, which smells spicy in the morning. "You just pay no attention to all that sensationalism, Eliza, and be your own sweet, happy self — okay?"

When he and Mom started talking about their evening plans for an out-of-town client, I excused myself almost silently and got away.

Robin and I talked about the news on the way to school. Miss Dixon's parents and her three brothers had come home from Wyoming and she wasn't with them. The police were staying in constant touch with them and they were ready to do anything to be helpful. Miss Dixon's father was shown at a fence with cows behind it, and he was wearing overalls and a cowboy hat. Her mother looked worried enough to cry. Her brothers were all the size of the barn behind them.

I didn't pay any attention to school all that morning. Mr. Heron came in again and managed to use up a whole lot of words to say nothing except that Miss Dixon was still missing and that they were sparing no effort in their search for her. We were not to be unduly concerned. I hate that expression "unduly concerned." After he left, the substitute teacher started trilling at us about our fascinating new study unit on Argentina.

Didn't they know this was the third day and nobody had even come up with any new ideas?

I wished that there was some way I could get out of going to lunch. It was taco day. Tacos taste good but they leak. They are particularly designed to dribble orange juice down your arms and stain the elbows of your shirts. Mom has fits about greasy orange elbow stains on my good clothes.

I knew I would only sit there picking out the tomato and cheese shreds and listening to a lot of stupid talk from my once-upon-a-time friends.

Perky leaned forward and started it. "Did you really knock Ben Hardy out?" she asked, keeping her voice down because Ben walked past the table just as she spoke.

"Down, not out," I told her. "And I don't want to talk about that. I want to talk about looking for Miss Dixon."

"Did Ben tell you where he got the dead mouse?" Patrick asked, as if he hadn't even heard me. "I never see dead mice. I don't even see live ones very much."

"At least not since last Friday," Perky said, giggling.

"Stop that!" I said. I could feel myself getting madder all the time. I hate to think of myself as an angry person. And when other people get mad, my stomach aches. But here it was halfway through Wednesday, and I had been angry the whole week so far.

"It's funny that I don't see more mice dead along the highway," Patrick mused. "I see all kinds of other road-kill — possums, raccoons, even squirrels, and they move really fast."

"Please," Perky said, deliberately gagging. "Some of us are eating." She was the only one who laughed.

"I remembered that I've seen her bike," Robin broke in. "It's black, with a carrier on the back and one of those woven-wire locks."

"Sst," Perky hissed, her eyes twinkling. "Tone it down. Ben Hardy is coming by here for the second time. I think he's trying to eavesdrop on us. Come on, Eliza, get up and knock him down."

"That's not funny," I said. "None of you are funny and it doesn't help to know what color her bike is unless we know where she rides it."

Chris gave a little gasp and looked at me with his mouth open. "Wow," he said. "I just remembered something. Last Saturday, Dad and I were driving out to his lab and having a very illuminating discussion about black holes. When Dad interrupted our talk to ask me if I could ride a bike without hands, I looked up. He was watching this biker go along the road ahead of us. It was Miss Dixon."

"Miss Dixon riding her bike with no hands?"

Patrick asked. Perky laughed but nobody paid any attention to her.

Chris nodded. "It really was her all right, with that same Nikon camera that usually sits on her desk."

"But where?" I asked, getting all excited again.

Chris stared at me with those strange pale eyes of his. "Out by the forest preserve on the west side of town," he said. "You know, the one that runs along there by Dad's lab."

"Now we just need to go out there after school and see if she had an accident or something," I said.

"In the rain?" Perky squealed. "I nearly drowned last night."

"Keep your voice down," Stephen warned as Ben drifted back toward the cafeteria line again. "Anyway, the rain's already slackening off."

Patrick shook his head. "I'd really love to go, but I have my paper route on Wednesdays."

"And I have a class in computer programming over at the junior college," Chris said.

"I can't go, either," Robin said, not looking up. "I coughed all last night and Mom made me swallow that awful cherry-tasting stuff."

I looked at them with their orange elbows and could actually see the pictures in one of my favorite nursery books. It was the story of a little red hen who wanted to make bread. Nobody would help her plant the wheat seed, and nobody would help her water the plants, grind the wheat into flour, or knead the dough. But they all lined up for nice hot pieces of bread when the loaf came out of the oven.

If that was the way they wanted it, that's what they would get. Stephen was the only one with a real excuse because he'd been forbidden to get involved, and he had already taken a lot of chances to help me. The rest of them made me sick. Why else should I feel as if I was going to barf when I had only eaten a few shreds of cheese?

Without even looking at them, I rose, dumped my plate into the garbage, and started out of the lunchroom. Robin called after me, but I didn't stop to find out what he was saying.

Ben Hardy had to move fast to do it, but he managed to step right in front of me as I reached the door.

"Think you're going somewhere?" he asked.

"I *know* I am," I shouted at him so loudly that the woman at the end of the cafeteria line looked over at us.

Ben glanced at the cafeteria attendant, made a rude noise in his throat, then stepped aside. The kids at my table weren't the only ones that started to laugh. I was glad someone enjoyed it because I knew I was going to pay for it someplace down the line.

All afternoon Robin and Stephen kept trying to

get my attention. I didn't look at them. Robin always coughs to get me to look at him. That afternoon he did it so many times that the substitute asked if he needed to visit the school nurse. When the last bell finally rang, I went straight to the pay phone outside the office. By moving fast, I was sure I could leave a message on the machine before Mom got home from the library to answer the phone in person.

9
The Search

By the time I had hung up the phone and reached the bike rack, Robin and Chris and Stephen were all there waiting. I didn't even speak to them but just unlocked my bike to start off. Within a few yards, Chris caught up with me. His long hair stuck out from the sides of his helmet, almost covering his cheeks.

"I changed my plans and will sit in on tomorrow's class at the college," he told me. "This way I can show you exactly where we saw Miss Dixon biking."

Before I could even thank him, Robin was there on my other side. "Mom always figures I'm over at your house when I don't get home anyway," he said. "So what's so big about pneumonia?"

Then Stephen caught up on his bike, keeping even with Robin and grinning at me. "I'm curious, Eliza. What did you tell your mother?"

"That I had a project after school."

"Won't she find out that you lied and give you one of those awful talking-to's?"

"I *didn't* lie," I told him. "I didn't even tell her it was an after-school project. I just said I had a project after school. How about you? Are you sure you won't get into trouble?" As if we hadn't already taken all the chances in the world of that happening!

"Only if we manage to find Miss Dixon, and in that case it will be worth it." He laughed and speeded up to pull ahead.

The rain had stopped but the sky hadn't cleared. The biking was slow going. The puddles that slopped over into the road had left patches of mud that were slick with fallen leaves. Although there was still plenty of light along the road, it was dusky back under the shade of the trees when Chris finally stopped and held up his hand.

"Dad and I saw Miss Dixon riding along just about here," he said. He motioned toward a grove of trees that looked to me exactly like a hundred we had already passed.

"How stupid can I get?" Steve asked, peering into the woods. "Why didn't I think about how much shade there is out here? A flashlight would sure be handy to look for bike tracks on the ground."

"First off, we need to find a trail where she could have gone off the road into the preserve,"

Chris said. "It'll only be a break in the fence with a path leading off."

I walked my bike around the puddles, looking for a place to get through the fence. Robin found the opening first and called for the rest of us to follow. He had gone only a few feet before he stopped.

"This isn't going to work," he called back. "The trail is nothing but mud. I can't even get my bike to go."

"Then we'll just have to lock the bikes all together here on the fence," Stephen said. "We've come too far to go back now."

Once away from the road, the woods became noisy. The rain dripping onto the forest floor made a steady drumming in the background. Small birds flitted and chirped nervously in the bushes. There was nothing nervous about the squirrels. They leaped from branch to branch, scolding us so loudly that only once in a while did we hear the barking of a deep-voiced dog coming from somewhere deep in the woods. Twigs snapped and a company of crows cawed furiously in the distance.

"I mean this is eerie," Robin grumbled. "I feel like a million eyes are watching us every minute."

"Don't even say stuff like that," I protested. "It gives me goose bumps."

"I know exactly what he means," Stephen said. "I feel the same way. But a lot of animals live in here. Even though I know that, I keep wanting

84

to look around, thinking I'll catch somebody following us."

He paused and squatted in the wet grass. After a minute he rose with a grunt of annoyance. "Boy, what I wouldn't give to know what Miss Dixon's bike treads looked like! Here are some bike tracks that go right off into the brush where's there's no path at all."

I stopped beside him and knelt down by the tracks. One good thing about the rain. It had made the earth soft enough to show faint bike tracks. Whoever had made the tracks had walked the bike along the trail. Leaves were smashed into the mud beside the bike tracks and even some small branches had been broken off the low bushes by whoever walked beside the bike.

"Are you game to follow this track off into the woods?" Stephen asked me. When I nodded, not trusting my voice to answer, he grinned at me. "The New Eliza," he said. His tone was teasing but kind of proud at the same time.

Chris and Robin fell in behind us and we walked in silence a little while, just looking and watching.

"I can't tell what I'm stepping on," Robin complained. "These twisted limbs look just like snakes."

"It's getting pretty cold now," Chris observed in a calm scientific tone. "Does anyone happen to know at what temperature a snake is too sluggish to strike?"

Robin moaned at his words and I shivered. It

was bad enough that the barking dog sounded closer the farther we walked, without people talking about snakes. Some little animal I couldn't see skittered off in the underbrush along the path. When I looked after it, pale green orbs of eyes shone at me from the bushes.

When something bigger grunted and scrambled away, startling me, I gasped and grabbed at Stephen. He laughed softly. "Just be afraid of the big ones who *don't* run away," he told me. "There aren't any animals out here bigger than skunks and you *want* them to run away!"

The ground had been rising gradually so that we had come to the top of a small hill. The crows who had cawed at a distance were suddenly very close, circling the woods around us. I tried not to think of that awful picture of crows that Miss Dixon had put on the bulletin board. Their cries sounded as angry and ferocious as they had looked, with their sharp beaks open and their wings spread wide.

"Do crows ever attack people?" I asked.

"Just other birds and small animals," Chris said. "Maybe dead people. They do eat carrion."

"Dead people," Robin repeated in a miserable voice. "What with snakes and dead people I'm ready to give up and go back."

"Look!" Chris cried suddenly. "There are lights up ahead. Strange lights, just flashing through the trees. Back and forth, back and forth." His voice sounded dreamy, the way it gets when he goes off on his wild space-travel talk.

"Don't start on that science fiction craziness, Chris," Stephen broke in crossly. "Those are car lights. Some are heading east and the others west. We've come clear through the preserve. That should be Highway 55 up ahead and it's just regular traffic. And there's the little farm below."

"Ouch," Robin cried. "And thorns. Watch out, you all, I just hit some mean thorns."

I had scratched myself, too. When I put my hand to my mouth I tasted blood. "I don't think these are thorns," I said. "Feel very carefully. There's barbed wire stretched along between the trees here."

"Who would put up barbed wire here?" Robin asked. "I thought this was all public property."

"Some of the people who owned property before the land became a forest preserve got to keep it," Stephen explained. "They owned just houses or a little acreage." He stopped beside me to stare into the hollow below.

"It looks more like a dump than anything else," Chris said. "Look at that mess down there. There's nothing but old vehicles and shanties and tumbledown buildings."

"And that crazy dog," Robin said. "He must be tied inside down there. I mean I *hope* he's tied inside."

The crows wheeled above us, practically drowning out our voices and the frantic barking of the dog. I started down into the hollow. I wished I hadn't been such a coward and had studied Miss Dixon's picture more closely. It didn't really look like a dump but more like an abandoned farm. Between us and a shanty-like building were some woodpiles and the shell of a rusted truck. An old van without any wheels had been set up on blocks out in back of the shanty. "Would we be trespassing if we just went down there to look around for Miss Dixon?" I asked.

"I can't imagine her going through this barbed wire and down that hill with her bike," Robin said.

"She could have parked her bike back there somewhere the way we did," I reminded him.

"Maybe," Chris said. "Why would she go down there anyway? There are plenty of leaves up here in the woods."

Robin made a strange little whimpering noise. "Okay, Okay," he said. "So I'm a wimp. That dog down there sounds big. I don't know about the rest of you all, but I'm freezing."

Stephen and I saw the car lights swerve in from the road at the same instant. The thought of that big dog coming after us really scared me. I whispered, "Everybody down. Flat."

I threw myself on the ground along with the others. I could feel my heart banging against the wet ground as I peered down the slope. We had gotten down just in time. The car that turned in was a station wagon, a big black one, with the rear windows covered with something like cardboard. The wagon ground over a high spot in the road, sweeping the top of the rise with a sudden flood of light. I heard Chris whistle softly with relief as the road leveled and the wagon pulled in to stop at the gate of the yard surrounding the shanty.

"Now what do we do?" Robin whispered, as a man got out of the car and opened the gate. He was a normal-sized person, wearing a worn-looking jean jacket and a baseball cap. His expression was what was scary. He looked back at the road and scowled as if he wanted to make sure that nobody was following them.

After a moment, he waved the driver through and closed the gate behind the station wagon. I caught my breath hard when the man driving then got out. He was giant-sized and heavyset as well. With his huge bushy dark beard and combat boots, he was twice as frightening to look at as his companion. After they had stood for a minute looking at the shanty, the big man said something I couldn't hear above the frantic barking of the dog. Then the smaller man ran ahead toward the shanty with the bigger one striding along behind him.

"We need to get to our bikes," I whispered, terrified that the big dog would come bounding out the minute they opened that door. "Stay down but get moving fast."

When Robin whimpered again, Stephen added, "Crawl!" in a fierce voice.

I'd never tried to crawl on my elbows backward but it was the fastest way. Just as I made it back in under the deep shade of the trees, I saw a light come on inside the shanty, glowing through smudged windows to throw pale patches on the ground outside.

Even over the outrage of the crows, I heard the dog's barking interspersed with yelps of welcome and heavy thumps as if he were hurling himself against a wall or cage.

"If they let that dog out, I will die right here in my tracks," Robin said, breathing heavily as he crawled through the brush. "Crow food, courtesy of Eliza Pharis."

Stephen turned on him swiftly. "Don't blame Eliza. We all came along of our own accord, remember? But you're right about one thing — they're bound to let the dog out to exercise. Run for the fence as fast as you can go."

We ran, breathless and panting, with the tree limbs clawing at us and the mud slippery and treacherous under our feet. Stephen had been right. They did let the dog out, and his voice changed as he bounded out of the shanty. He was growling fiercely as he plunged off into the woods as if he were after some enemy. Luckily for us, he went chasing off in the opposite direction.

Since it was getting close to suppertime, traffic

had picked up along the road where we had left our bikes. By running toward the traffic sounds, we reached the fence faster than I would have thought possible. We all collapsed on the sodden ground beside our bikes.

"I've never been so glad to leave any place in my life," Robin said, knocking at the mud on his bike wheels.

"We were lucky there was something in there besides us," Stephen said. "I'm just glad the dog went for it instead."

"As a matter of scientific interest, I'd like to know what it was," Chris added.

Right then I didn't care. I just wanted to be as far away from that place as I could get. I pedaled silently, fighting more than the weight of the mud on my wheels. I knew that was the same place Miss Dixon had gone for her pictures. It had all looked too familiar, the tree and the crows and those ragged little buildings beyond, just like the picture she had put on the bulletin board. We had gotten away from there, but had she?

I've never been so glad to see Mom's station wagon gone from the garage and the house dark. At least I'd have a chance to clean up before she saw me.

She had left a note propped against the plate of chocolate cookies on the kitchen table. "Sorry I missed you, Sweetie. I had to meet Dad and his client for dinner in town. You and Robin do your homework before you play. When you feel hungry, put something in the microwave. I expect to be back by eight at least."

Robin had gone on home to change his wet clothes. I sat a long time looking at the cookies. When I finally tried one, it tasted like brown chalk. I had never been so scared in my life. Neither had I ever been so discouraged.

We'd gone to the right place, I knew it. But I couldn't possibly ask my friends to put themselves through this again. I would have to do it on my own. The very thought made me feel cold to the bone.

I put the rest of the cookies back into the box so Mom wouldn't ask why Robin and I hadn't liked them. After putting my wet clothes in the laundry hamper, I took a hot shower and curled up in bed with my homework.

The phone rang three times before I went downstairs to answer it.

"You're not in bed already?" Stephen asked.

"Not to sleep," I said. "I was trying to read social studies but not getting very far with it."

"Then you didn't watch the news?"

That little twist of hope came up in my chest in spite of myself. I gripped the phone with both hands. "Do they know anything?" I asked breathlessly.

His voice was heavy with disgust. "Worse than that. The announcer said he called the school for a report on the missing teacher, but the principal didn't return his call."

I sighed. "Thanks for letting me know anyway," I said.

"One thing you might be interested in," he said quickly, as if he were afraid I might hang up. "They caught the man who was shaving all the English sheepdogs. Those animals had all won ribbons in a countywide show where his dog didn't even place."

"That's crazy," I told him.

"Like a fox," he said. "The local competition comes up right away. He figured this would make his dog a shoo-in."

He hesitated a moment, then said, "Eliza?"

When I answered, he went on swiftly. "I'm as sorry as anything about today. Do you want to cut school and go out there again tomorrow and try again?"

I caught my breath sharply at the thought. "I couldn't ask you to do that," I said.

"I just don't want you going out to that place alone, that's all. Hear me?"

I mumbled that I heard him. That wasn't the same as a promise, but it was enough to get him off the phone. When he was off the line, I stared at the phone for a long time. I really hadn't liked his tone very much. Who was he to tell me what he wanted me to do or not do?

10
Life Without Ben

That Thursday morning Ben Hardy's chair was empty. Right away I felt a sense of relief. Ever since I had knocked him down, a little shiver went up my spine when I thought of him. No matter what Stephen said, Ben would get even. It was just a matter of time.

It also cheered me that the morning newscaster had expressed "extreme" concern about the continuing failure of the local police to discover the whereabouts of Miss Gretchen Dixon. A number of local residents had called the station to protest the lackadaisical handling of the case and discuss the rising concern among her students. I figured that Dad really had called, and I wasn't sorry, either.

The newscaster also reported that the police planned to search the missing teacher's home for clues to where she might be.

The same substitute teacher was back and bubbling over with good spirits again. At least she

94

had the excuse of a nice sunny day. I made myself concentrate all morning to try to overcome my awful sense of panic. Thursday! Four days. If Miss Dixon had been in a bike accident, she could have starved to death by now, or died without water, or maybe bled to death.

The sunshine did help. That morning might have been reasonably pleasant if I had been able to forget for one single minute that Miss Dixon was still missing.

I usually like the spaghetti at school, but that day the sauce was too thick and strong. Robin made a face at me over his first bite because he likes my mother's sauce even better than the kind his mother buys in jars. Stephen looked at me suspiciously while I pushed the red strings around on my plate. "You're not planning to do anything foolish, are you?" he asked.

"Do I look especially foolish today?" I asked.

"Every day lately," he grumbled, still eyeing me.

Lucky for me Patrick changed the subject. "I heard on the news that the police caught a Peeping Tom," Patrick said. "Did your dad do that, Stephen?"

Stephen shook his head. "No, but the whole force was glad to get it over with. It was a silly mistake in the first place. The phone kept ringing with reports of this man looking into upstairs windows at twilight. It wasn't even a man at all. It

95

was only one of the high school kids practicing stilt-walking after school for an amateur talent show."

"Oh, wow," Robin said, almost choking on his spaghetti. "I never thought of trying that. How to get tall without even growing!"

"Watch the news tonight," Stephen said. "Dad says that freaky local newscaster had a ball taking pictures of the stilt walker."

I poked at my plate. Great! The police could catch dog barbers and stilt walkers but they didn't have time to worry about a teacher who had disappeared into thin air. Would they even realize that the rotten hamburger was a clue that Miss Dixon meant to come back from wherever she was? I didn't care what Stephen thought about her forgetting the meat. She and I were not the kind of people who forget things like that.

Ben still hadn't come at the end of lunch hour. The substitute counted us off into special study groups to prepare reports on Argentina. There was grumbling and a lot of complaints that Miss Dixon never made us do that. The substitute just laughed and practically sang out her instructions to the groups.

"Can anyone just naturally be that hyper?" I asked Chris as he pulled up his chair beside mine.

"It's questionable," Chris said, nodding thoughtfully. "There's probably a scientific explanation. Maybe she reacts with ebullience to one of those mysterious gases that are seeping through our ozone layer. Those things can be invisible death."

"I think it's okay that *somebody* feels good," Robin said. "I feel awful." He had sniffled all day and his voice was beginning to sound rough and funny because he'd been wet and cold for two afternoons in a row. "And we can all be grateful that we don't have Ben to deal with today."

"There's your explanation for a happy teacher right there," Patrick whispered.

Miss Dixon had never assigned anything like this study group idea but at least it was distracting. Each group had four kids in it — three research people and one record keeper. Stephen and Patrick and I volunteered to do the research because Chris is the best on the computer.

When no one would volunteer to take any of the subjects the teacher had written on the board, she assigned them to the groups. I hoped our group would get animals. Instead we got climate and weather.

At least climate and weather sounded like an easy topic. What could weather really do except go from cold to hot and wet to dry and back again on both counts?

With three of us working, we got a lot of material together pretty fast. Chris, watching us, practically exploded with excitement, grinning out at us between those hunks of hair. "Look what we've got!" he cried. "We have climate ranging from subtropical in the north to cold and wind-swept in the southern regions, where Argentina claims a part of Antarctica. There's almost every kind of terrain in the world there."

"We'll never make sense of all this," Patrick wailed. "Just wait and see. We'll all flunk on this."

"Graphs," Chris cried. "We'll make graphs on the computer that show the percentages of the different climates. The line graphs of temperatures will be fantastic. We can make a pie to show the six separate geographical regions with their marshlands and grasslands and high plateaus and rain forests. We can mount an exhibit all the way across the top of the blackboard and still have pampas left over."

He was still bouncing up and down trying to explain how exciting it was when the substitute teacher called me up to her desk.

"Mr. Heron would like to see you in his office," she said quietly. I stared at her, trying to think what I could possibly have done. My mind was totally blank.

"I need to go to the office, too," Chris told her. "I need at least one new computer disk to put our Argentina report on."

She nodded her approval, then looked back at me. "Don't just stand there, Eliza," she said, letting her smile slip a little. "You run on down to the office with Chris."

Chris kept babbling on about bar graphs and programming all the way down the hall. The minute we got there, Miss Burns waved me toward Mr. Heron's inner office. "You go right in," she told me. "He's waiting."

Mr. Heron was not alone. A large woman wearing blue slacks under a short white coat was all humped over in his extra chair. When Ben Hardy's mother, her face puffy and red from crying and her hair every which way, twisted around to glare at me, I knew right then why I had been sent for.

"There she is," she said, pointing right at me. "Ask her if she didn't hit my boy. Ask her if she didn't knock him down so hard that the poor child could hardly walk Tuesday after he got home."

I must have looked awful because Mr. Heron's voice was actually gentle when he spoke to me. "Eliza," he said quietly. "We seem to have a problem here. Mrs. Hardy tells me that you and Ben had some trouble on the school grounds Tuesday afternoon. Is that the case?"

I forced myself to look him in the face. "Yes sir."

"And do I understand that you struck Ben, knocking him down?"

I nodded before I got the words out. "Yes, sir, I did."

He leaned forward a little, staring at me with his eyes very wide open. "You did what?"

"I hit Ben Hardy in the face and knocked him down on the playground after school on Tuesday," I said, all in one big breath.

"What in the world made you do that?" He sounded as astonished as I had felt when I did it.

"He swung a dead mouse in my face." My voice kept fading in and out like a badly tuned radio.

"A typical childish prank," Mrs. Hardy broke in angrily. "Nothing for her to turn violent about."

Violent would be the word mothers would use, too.

"Please, Mrs. Hardy," Mr. Heron said. "Let Eliza give us her own account of what happened between her and Ben." He sounded understanding, but he folded his hands together on the desk the way he did when he was about to announce a major punishment.

I especially remembered seeing him do that when some third graders had started a snowball fight with my second-grade class out behind the school. The minute after those third graders started throwing their snowballs, they all ran away. We hadn't realized they were standing in front of the library windows. We were pretty good throwers for second grade. We knocked out three windows before we could stop ourselves.

Mr. Heron was still waiting for my full account of what happened.

"Ben told me that Miss Dixon had been found,"

I said. "Then he swung a dead mouse in my face and I hit him."

"This is not making sense to me," the principal said, shaking his head. "Ben said that Miss Dixon had been found? Why would he say that? Here it is Thursday and regrettably we still have no word of her whereabouts. And what in the world has a dead mouse to do with all of this?"

"That's what Ben always called Miss Dixon," I explained. "He nicknamed her 'the Mouse' the very first day and had all the other kids calling her that, too. And she wasn't mousy at all. She was a wonderful teacher."

"A typical childish trick," Mrs. Hardy said. "Children always give nicknames to other people." Mr. Heron glanced at her then turned back to me.

"Do you know where Ben Hardy is today?" he asked.

I stared at him. There was warning in his tone. Could I have really hurt Ben when I knocked him down? He couldn't be sick in the hospital, sick and about to die because of me.

I shook my head wildly. "He can't be hurt. He was prowling around eavesdropping on us kids yesterday at lunch."

"But have you seen him today?" Mr. Heron asked.

I shook my head. "He's not in class," I whispered, avoiding Mrs. Hardy's angry eyes. "That's all I know. He's not in class."

"He's missing, that's what he is," she broke in. "Run away for all I know. No telling what kind of awful place he's ended up in. The poor little fellow had all he could take of you kids making fun of him and picking on him, even knocking him down and splitting his lip so it bled. I just know you made life so miserable for him yesterday that he couldn't face it anymore."

I could only stare at her.

"We haven't seen hair of him since yesterday morning when he set off for school," Mrs. Hardy went on, beginning to cry again.

"And you have no idea where Ben might be?" Mr. Heron asked me, "or where he might have gone?"

When I shook my head, he looked at me thoughtfully for a minute. "Did anyone else see this happen?" he asked.

I nodded. "Stephen Zloty was with me."

He rose and put his hand on my shoulder, nudging me toward the outer office. "Don't go back to your class yet, Eliza. I want to hear what Stephen has to say about this."

There wasn't any sign of Chris, but I didn't look back into the storeroom. Since there wasn't any place for me to sit down I went out into the hall. I leaned against the wall outside and watched Miss Burns go toward the fifth-grade room. In a minute she was going to come back out with Stephen. If Stephen passed me looking sympathetic, I knew

I would break out bawling. The only place to hide was in the girls' washroom, and I barely made it in there in time.

I stood in the middle of the dim washroom that smelled of those awful blue chemicals they put in the toilets. A little pool of half-dried yellow soap had leaked from the dispenser down onto one of the basins. When I looked in the mirror, my face looked watery where somebody had smudged the glass. I heard voices in the hall but I couldn't make out any words.

All I could hear were Mrs. Hardy's words. Violent. Missing. Run away. No telling what kind of awful place.

And my own voice lying even though I hadn't known it was a lie at the time.

Mr. Heron had asked, "And you have no idea where Ben might be? Or where he might have gone?"

I knew. Of course I knew. We had all watched Ben traipse back and forth spying on us while we talked about going out to the forest preserve. We had all talked about having that feeling that someone was following us, that someone or something was watching us.

Ben. That had to be Ben. It had to be Ben that the barking dog had run after when the men let him out of the shanty. Had the same kind of terrible thing happened to Miss Dixon? Were both of them out there lying bleeding or dead maybe?

Whatever had happened to Ben was all my fault. Nobody else had even wanted to go out there. I'd been as much a bully as Ben himself, making everybody feel rotten unless they did what I wanted done. And all to no good end. I hadn't helped Miss Dixon at all, and now I had maybe hurt another kid, too.

The latch on the washroom door squealed a little when I opened it. The hall was empty and quiet. I didn't even go to my locker for fear someone would see me. I had to stop at home for a flashlight anyway, in case the woods were dark again. I could also grab another warm jacket.

I was already crying when I fumbled the lock off my bike and started for home. The sky was clouding over and I shivered in the wind. I didn't even feel angry and violent anymore. I just felt sick and scared and sorry down in my bones for all the things I had done wrong when I had only wanted to help somebody I really liked.

11
Simple Simon

The clouds were thick and curdled-looking by the time I got home. It was stupid and careless of me but I didn't pay much attention to what I was doing. Once inside, I pushed Simon out of my way and told him to be a good boy because I was in a hurry. It only took a minute to run down and get Dad's big flashlight off his workbench and grab my old goose down parka off the hook inside the back door.

Within a block, I was glad I had the hooded parka because it began to sprinkle in that lazy way that usually doesn't amount to anything. I took the shortest route I could take without going close to my school. I was almost to the edge of town when I reached the first stoplight on red.

I heard Simon before I saw him. He had been galloping after me all the way from home and only caught up because I had stopped. The light turned green and back to red while I tried to decide what to do. Simon is big and beautiful and I love him dearly, but he has the brains of a fruit fly. The only way to get him back home would be to catch him and drag him there. By that time, the splattering rain could turn the forest preserve into a streaming darkness.

"All right, you great big dummy," I told him. "Just remember this was *your* idea."

When we reached that stretch of country road that runs by the forest preserve, I panicked. All the groves of trees still looked just as much alike to me as they had the day before. I slowed down, peering at the woods, trying desperately to remember one single landmark at the place we had gone in. Simon loped along beside me, dragging a little after the high-speed race from town.

Finally, I gave up. As I stood staring helplessly into the woods, Simon lifted his head, gave a happy woof, and bounded on down the road ahead of me.

When I tried to call him back, Chris called to me from the road up ahead. "That's okay, Eliza, I got him. What took you so long?"

I never had so many tears come so fast in my life. I ran toward him not even caring that I was blubbering like a baby. "Chris," I wailed. "How come? How did you know?"

"It is in the nature of the scientist to be curious," he told me. "When I saw Mrs. Hardy in that office, I employed the ancient scientific technique of rolled tube against wall to eavesdrop on what was going on. When I heard Ben's mother say he never made it home yesterday, I came to the same conclusion you did. I hope you didn't bring this animal in place of a torch."

I handed him the flashlight. "I didn't bring him, he came, and I'm afraid he'll be a problem down in those woods."

Chris nodded agreement. "If you can spare the belt off your jacket, maybe I can tie him to the fence."

When he finished securing the dog, he ordered Simon to sit and stay. I didn't say anything. Maybe Simon was too dumb to obey, but he was probably too worn out to try to follow us, either.

"I presume you have a plan," Chris said, leaning against the fence and staring off into the woods.

I shook my head, feeling awfully stupid. "Only that I had to get back out here to look for Ben. I wanted to get here earlier. It was later than this when those men in the station wagon drove in and let the dog out. I didn't get much of a look at them, but what I got scared me. The big bearded one looked the worst, but the little guy in the baseball hat had a mean tight mouth. Something was wrong about the way they looked and about their having that big dog penned up out here." The question had been hammering in my head all the way out from town. I couldn't ask it any louder than a whisper. "Chris, do guard dogs kill boys?"

His mouth twisted a little as if he was fighting

a grin. "Not usually," he said. "But don't discount a bully being scared to death."

"Don't say that," I wailed.

Chris frowned, listening to the cries of the crows coming from over the rise. "I don't hear the dog, do you?"

I shook my head. "But he only really got noisy when we were close to the shanty."

"Let's make our way down there from a different direction," Chris suggested thoughtfully. "Remember that old van out in back? If we cut around and came in behind it, we could get a lot closer without the risk of being seen."

We made a wide arc to the left of the path we had followed the day before. At least the rain came and went in lazy little showers instead of really drowning us. The woods were wet enough already and loud with birds. Once in a while I heard Simon whimper from up by the fence, but mostly the noises came from the crows and the woods themselves. The dog that had barked the day before was still silent.

I followed closely after Chris, fighting loose brush that snagged and tangled around my feet. Suddenly, something sharp whipped around my ankle and tightened against my leg. I gasped and would have screamed but Chris caught my arm.

"What's wrong? What happened?" he asked.

"Snakes!" I whispered unable to make myself move. "My leg." I stood frozen while he knelt beside me. When he caught something that tightened like a noose against my jeans leg, I put both fists in my mouth to keep from screaming.

"Snake indeed!" Chris said, sounding suddenly jovial. He rose and dangled something slender and shiny in front of me. "This rare specimen is of the genus Photographicus. Unlike the pit viper, which responds to heat, it is activated by light."

I stared at it in disbelief. Film. A curled length of 35-millimeter film. "Miss Dixon," I breathed, my heart starting to bang hard all over again.

"I felt better before we found this," he admitted, looping the exposed film into a bundle as he went down on his knees. "Flash the light around low, Eliza, back and forth here on the ground."

We were both on our knees by the time we found Miss Dixon's Nikon. It had been smashed into a number of pieces against a good-sized rock. Chris found the telescopic lens, tucked it into his pocket, and stood up.

"This does it. We're not looking at any accident," he said. "We need to go back to the road, try to stop a car, and get some kind of sensible help."

I knew he was right but we were so close. "Couldn't we just get a little closer to that shanty?" I asked. "She could be hurt in there."

He studied me for a long moment, then nodded. "One quick look," he agreed, "then out of here like a shot." He took my arm as we edged forward.

109

We passed the wrecked van and crept toward the broken-down house. Because of the rain and the coming dusk, some of the highway drivers had turned on their lights. The lights flashed eerily through the woods around us. We were only a few feet from the shanty when something startled the crows into one of those sudden bursts of horrid cawing. I yelped in spite of myself but covered my mouth at once.

I think we were both holding our breath when we heard the thumping from inside the shanty. I caught Chris's arm hard.

"Let's try not to use the light," he whispered. "I'll try the door." The lock was just a big piece of flat board that fitted through a wooden slot. I didn't understand why we hadn't heard the dog. Maybe he had made the thumping noise in there. Maybe he would lunge out of that door the minute Chris worked the big wooden bar loose.

"I can't do it alone," Chris whispered. I put down the flashlight and used both hands to push against the bar along with him. It still wouldn't move with both of us putting our whole weight against it.

"Come on, you stupid thing," I whispered. "Let's hit it again on a count of three."

The bar finally loosened with an angry squeak. The thumping started again inside the cabin, with strange muffled cries.

I picked up my flashlight and together we

pushed the heavy wooden door open just a few inches. The little bit of light that came through the filthy windows didn't help make sense of the place.

Rubble was strewn all over the floor, but something was neatly stacked against one wall. Chris grabbed the flashlight and played the beam along the line of boxes against the wall.

He whistled softly and whispered, "So that's what this is all about."

"What's what all about?" I asked, staring at the boxes. I only saw the letter K, with some symbols after it, before Chris doused the light.

"Potassium chlorate," Chris said. "The chemicals that were stolen last week. Your instincts were right about those guys. We better get out of here, fast."

All the things I had heard flashed through my mind — explosives used by terrorists, blowing up planes, banks.

"But the thumping," I reminded him. He knelt and played the light low around the room. The place didn't even have a floor but was just a jumble of boards torn loose and thrown every which way. Where the corner of the room should have been was only a gaping hole. The noise I kept hearing was coming from down there. Something was moving down in that hole, twisting and grunting and making pitiful muffled cries.

Chris and I knelt at the edge of the depression

and shone the light down. Ben Hardy was curled up with his knees tied in front of his chest and his arms bound in back. His eyes were terrified and pleading as he tried to shove himself up toward us.

Chris dropped down and jerked the filthy gag away from Ben's mouth. "I'm dying," Ben wailed. "Help me! Undo my legs."

When Chris and I tried to help him up, he let out a yell. "Careful!" he cried. "My leg is all chewed up and bloody. But we've got to get out of here fast. Those guys have been loading those boxes out there, but they're not through. They could be back for another pile any minute."

12
Flight

Even in the dim light of the shanty, we could see the torn place in Ben's jeans with blood matted darkly all around it. While I tugged and groped at Ben's rope, he snorted and groaned and gasped right in my face so that I could hardly breathe. Seeing how much trouble I was having, Chris took a stab at it.

I couldn't bear just standing there, watching him. I kept seeing those men's faces and how scary they had looked to me as I crawled backward up that wet hill. We had to get out of there, all three of us. I didn't want to be caught in there with any men who would steal potentially dangerous chemicals like that and tie up a kid like Ben.

"Give it up, Chris," I said. "Let's clear a path so we can take Ben out of here." He looked startled but jumped to his feet at once. We started across the room toward the door like a couple of crazies, kicking and shoving lumber and rubble out of our way.

"Come on, Ben," I called back to him. "Start rolling yourself toward that door."

"But my leg," Ben wailed. "That dog nearly chewed it off. Every time I move, it hurts."

"I know that," Chris said. "You want to be here when he comes back again? If not, quit whining and get moving," Chris ordered, giving him a shove.

I felt sorry for Ben with his leg all bitten, but I knew Chris and I were right. While we cleared a path through the trash, Ben, groaning at every move, rolled and bumped to the doorway.

The steps were the worst. Chris and I braced him going down onto the level ground but that was all. "Get yourself moving," Chris told him. "Get as far away as possible, back toward that van." Chris's voice was crisp with command. "You, Eliza, come grab this door."

The door weighed a ton and kept hanging up on the wet sill. My arms ached by the time we finally got it into place. We had the bolt only halfway through the slot when a set of lights turned in from the road.

"We can't make a run for it with Ben tied up like that," I said, suddenly panicked again.

"Then we hide," Chris said. "We ought to be able to fit under that old van."

Except for the time I knocked him down in the schoolyard, I had never laid a hand on Benjamin Hardy. I knew he was big, but I didn't have any

114

idea how much a kid like that could weigh. By the time Chris and I dragged him in under the shadow of the van, we were both panting.

I knew we weren't really safe there. And in a way it was worse than the day before because we couldn't see anything. We didn't dare creep close enough to the side of the old van to try to watch what was going on. I heard the gate open and the station wagon pull into the drive.

The dog must have come back with the men because I heard him whine as the men pulled up to the front of the shanty. Would they notice right off that the bolt was not shoved in all the way? We could only lie there trying not to breathe that moldy air and listen to the crows screaming in the tops of the trees. "What will they do when they find him missing?" I breathed to Chris.

"Be scientific," he whispered back. "Cross your fingers."

Ben kept rustling loudly behind us. "What do you think you're doing?" I whispered crossly. "Be quiet."

"This cement block has a sharp edge," Ben whispered. "I'm working on my ropes. If they set that dog on us, we're dead."

Chris nudged me. "He could have something there," he said. "You go get up into the van, Eliza," he whispered. "Ben and I will follow you."

I gasped, then scrambled out from under the back side of the van and pulled myself up through the half-open door. I bit my lip hard to keep from squealing when something warm and sleek rubbed past me, escaping from the torn upholstery of the driver's seat. Crouching down, I edged backward to make room for Chris and Ben if they ever got those ropes free.

Then everything happened at once.

Ben whispered, "There!" in a note of triumph, and I heard him and Chris clawing their way up into the van behind me.

The men's voices sounded awfully close as they exploded in a roar of angry curses. I heard something slam like the door of the shanty being thrown back against the outside wall, and one of the men yelled, "The brat is gone!"

"He can't be far," the other man called back. A shrill whistle pierced the air and he called to the dog. "Here, boy! Go get him, boy!"

The three of us crouched together behind the front seat of the van, hardly breathing. The dog barked, then yipped as if the man had struck him with something. The man cursed at him.

I knew then it was all over. If the men didn't find us, the dog would. I could almost feel the fury of the men battering us inside that dark little van. I heard the dog snuffling close to the open door of the van, and I cringed closer to the floor.

Suddenly, in the middle of that awful uproar, one of the men shouted, "Look out!" and screamed. It was a high shrill sound as if he were in sudden and terrible pain. His screech died in a curse and he began yelling again, this time shouting for help.

"Get a light!" he howled. "Get this devil off me. Club him!"

The confusion of sounds made absolutely no sense at all. It sounded as if a whole pack of dogs was out there, all fighting each other. I caught my breath hard as the deep baying of the guard dog ended in a yelp followed by a heavy throaty snarl.

Chris pressed his mouth close to my ear. "Simon," he breathed.

It was as if someone had hit me in the chest. Simon! That couldn't be right. I had to believe Chris was wrong. How could Simon have gotten loose from that fence? How did he know to find us here? Simon wasn't a fighter, he was a big, simple, loving animal. Whatever dogs were out there would tear him to shreds.

But I knew my dog's voice too well. That *was* Simon out there taking on that awful dog and those dreadful men with no help from anybody.

I hadn't cried. I hadn't even whimpered through all that horror. But the thought of poor, simple, good-natured Simon trying to fend off that vicious dog and those men with clubs was more than I could handle. I don't really know what I meant to do — maybe help Simon, maybe just get the whole thing over, no matter how it ended. As I leaped to climb over that van seat, Chris caught me and jerked me back. I heard my head crack against the side of the door and felt a sudden dizziness from pain.

I blinked and moaned as everything turned strange. Suddenly, it was like science fiction and the world of Chris and his crazy alien beings. The woods were flooded with light that angled in through the van's shattered windows. I heard a voice like thunder — or at least like that of an announcer at a football game — shouting words I couldn't make out over the snarling of the dogs and the wild cawing of the crows.

Then, over the yelling, I heard someone crashing through the woods past the van. A motor was kicked into life. It either backfired or there were gunshots as it roared away from the shanty, slammed through the gate, and sped onto the road, tires screaming.

Then Stephen was there, calling to me. I recognized his voice instantly. "Eliza," he called. "Chris, Eliza, where are you?"

Ben got his voice back first, but without real words. "Jeeminy," he gasped. "Jeeminy whiz!"

Chris untangled himself and started climbing toward the door. "Here we are," he called to Stephen. "Inside this van."

When Stephen appeared at the broken door, his father loomed behind him. Stephen was babbling,

"You all right? You okay?" as his father shone a flashlight in on us, moving from my face to Chris's and then to Ben's.

I know I was babbling, too, as the beam of light moved past us to play around the interior of the van. When I saw Stephen's eyes widen in astonishment, I turned to look, too.

Miss Dixon, trussed the way Ben had been, was staring back at us from the shadowy darkness of the back of the van. Her eyes were wide and tearful above the gag that half covered her face.

Suddenly, there wasn't room for all of us in that cluttered space. Mr. Zloty thrust the flashlight at Stephen and got through that door in seconds. For a big man, he could sure move fast. "You kids clear out of here," he ordered, clambering over the debris toward Miss Dixon.

Ropes are easier to undo when you have a knife. He had Miss Dixon free and on her feet within minutes, then helped her out onto the ground. She looked really tiny next to Mr. Zloty. He had to help her walk because she had been tied up too long for her legs to work yet.

I would die before I would tell Benjamin Hardy this, but she *really* looked like a mouse right then. Her face was pale and thinner from all those days of imprisonment. And her nose looked more pointed because it was red from crying. That was okay. She had every right to cry and I did, too. I cried because she was still alive and not all bashed up like her camera. And I cried extra because she and I are the same kind of people. I knew how angry and helpless she must have felt lying there all tied up and not able to do what she knew she was supposed to be doing.

She didn't even try to talk until she was outside, leaning against Mr. Zloty and struggling for breath. "What happened? I don't understand any of this," she asked, her words coming separately as if she still wasn't getting enough air. "How did you ever find me?"

Mr. Zloty twisted his mouth in a funny way, then stretched his neck as if he had a crick in it. "I wish I could claim finding you," he said, "but I've got to give the credit to these kids. I only came because my kid dragged me and convinced me that their theories were better than ours. Once we got in that apartment of yours, we knew you had meant to come back there right away."

"He still kept threatening me every mile of the way," Stephen said, grinning at me. "He kept calling this a wild-goose chase that I was going to live to regret."

Mr. Zloty smiled, too. "The real wild goose is Eliza Pharis here. She's been badgering the world to find you since Monday. This kid doesn't know how to give up."

I tried to meet Miss Dixon's eyes but couldn't. "How did you know? Why did you come?" she asked, her eyes on my face, wondering.

I shrugged. "You told us about the leaves for the November bulletin board," I stammered. "Chris and his dad had seen you riding out here Saturday. I knew this was the right place because of the crow pictures. And I knew you would be at school if you could get there."

"Oh, Eliza," she said, making a funny little face. "I'm never going to be able to thank you. And I hope I go the rest of my life without ever hearing a single crow call."

A siren whined, coming steadily closer. While we were talking, two other policemen that I hadn't even seen had walked up to the side of the van to speak quietly to Mr. Zloty.

He whistled, then turned to Miss Dixon again. "There'll be all kinds of time for talk after you're taken care of," Mr. Zloty said. "For now, let's get you down to that access road for the ambulance I ordered."

She shook her head. "I need some explanations right now. I haven't any idea what this is all about. I was working my way through the woods to get down to that grove of oak trees to take some pictures when two men jumped out at me. I tried to get away but the big one was too strong for me. He held me while the smaller man broke my camera and ripped out all my exposed film. What was I doing wrong? Why did they tie me up in there all that time?"

"It was probably your camera they were afraid

of," Mr. Zloty said. "They're thieves. They probably thought you had stumbled onto their temporary storage place for a potential fortune in chemicals, especially potassium chlorate, that would bring a fancy price in the criminal market. According to my men, even with what they have managed to move out, that shanty still holds a sizable amount of their loot. We've had a desperate search on for those chemicals since they were stolen from a local plant nearly a week ago."

"Chris saw what it was right off," I told them. "All I saw was the letter K."

"The symbol for the element potassium," Miss Dixon said, her voice thoughtful. Her eyes suddenly widened. "What were they going to do to me?"

"And me," Ben piped up, his voice very high and squeaky.

Mr. Zloty shrugged. "The first thing they were after was to wreck your camera. They were right. That was the smartest move they could have made. Good clear pictures would have given us the kind of evidence they couldn't refute. Once the film was destroyed, they only had to pin you and Ben down until they could load the stuff out of that shack. What they would have done with you two then is anybody's guess."

The ambulance attendant insisted that Miss Dixon lie down on a stretcher. She obeyed him, then rose on one elbow and looked back at us. Her face was dirty and her shiny brown hair was matted from being pressed back under her gag, but I recognized a look in her eyes as a feeling I had thought belonged only to me.

I stepped forward without even thinking about it. "You don't want to go there all by yourself," I told her.

She smiled with the edges of her mouth turned down a little. "You're right, Eliza, I don't," she whispered, catching my hand in hers to take me along.

13
The New Eliza

It felt strange to follow Miss Dixon's stretcher into the emergency room and hear her insist that I stay with her. "Eliza can fill out the forms," she told the woman with the clipboard while one nurse took her blood pressure and another clocked her pulse. "I'll tell her what to put down."

The woman didn't trust me to do it. As she began answering the questions, Miss Dixon winked at me as if to say that *we* knew I could have handled it. Miss Dixon winced just the way I always do when they take blood samples.

When the nurse asked Miss Dixon what she had been given to eat and drink, Miss Dixon sat straight up on her hospital bed. Her eyes snapped with anger. "Junk food and water," she said, shaking her head at the memory. "Greasy meat and greasy potatoes and more of the same. I'll never put another hamburger in my mouth as long as I live!"

The nurse made her lie back down and sent for

a tray. By the time Miss Dixon had eaten a dish of custard, along with a bowl of fruit and some Jell-O, she began to look more like herself.

"Mr. Zloty would like to speak to you when you feel like it," the nurse told her.

"I really think I'm fine," Miss Dixon told her.

Stephen's father made the small curtained room shrink to almost nothing. He stood at the foot of Miss Dixon's bed, looking first at me and then at her. "You're looking pretty good," he told her.

"I'm a biker," she said. "We stay in shape."

Mr. Zloty had a clipboard, too. He took it out, snapped open his pen, and looked over at me again. "Your folks have been pretty nearly frantic about you, Eliza. I phoned them and said that you were here and all right. They're on their way over now. Wouldn't you like to go out and wait for them?"

"I think Eliza would rather wait in here," Miss Dixon said. "She's spent all this time wondering why I didn't make it to class."

Mr. Zloty smiled and turned to her. "We got your folks pretty upset during our search for you, too. I called them and promised you'd talk to them yourself later tonight."

She thanked him and grinned at me as he began questioning her.

What Miss Dixon said answered most of my questions, too. When Chris and his dad had seen her on Saturday, she was going to the preserve hoping to get pictures of colored autumn leaves. When she found that not many leaves had survived the rain, she started taking photographs of the shapes of different varieties of trees.

"I was snapping that grove of oaks down by the shanty when I realized that these men were standing down there, watching me. Since they looked as if they resented my trespassing, I went back to my bike and came home."

"That was Saturday?" Mr. Zloty asked. "But you went back?"

"On Sunday," she said, nodding. "I had spoiled my tree pictures by getting those men and their station wagon in the shot. I went back hoping to get the grove by itself."

Mr. Zloty sighed. "What I wouldn't give for that roll of film they tore out of your camera and destroyed. It could have all the identification we need."

She shook her head. "I didn't get a chance to take any pictures Sunday. The film they destroyed was a brand-new roll. I had already developed the ones I took Saturday. That's how I knew I had to go back."

He was still staring at her, speechless, when the nurse stuck her head in between the curtains. "Eliza Pharis," she said, "your parents are here for you."

Not until that moment did I ever stop to wonder how my parents were going to react to what had happened. I was almost stiff with fear as I walked out. They were standing very close together, staring at me as if I were a stranger.

Before I could catch my breath, my mother had crossed the room to take me in her arms. She hugged me and kissed my face and hair, all the time whispering every sweet name she has ever called me. In between the "Sweeties" and "Babies," she kept asking over and over if I was really all right, if I had been hurt at all.

Somehow Dad had managed to get his arms around both of us and was carrying on the same way. Usually, I say I don't like sloppy, sentimental carrying on, but I guess I do way down deep. Being wrapped up in love like that wasn't silly at all but simply glorious.

But finally Mom released me to hold me away from her and smile. Dad became his old cool self at about the same moment. I knew there was explaining to do, and I wanted to do it right then while they were so warm with relief.

Mom didn't give me the chance. Instead, she took my arm and said, "Come on, Sweetie. I won't feel like this is over until we get you safely home."

I tried to start telling them about what had happened but Dad broke in, his voice already sounding more like the old Dad. "Never mind now, Eliza," he said. "We'll have a talk when we get home."

Have a talk? I guess I began to get scared again

right then. But this was different from other bad things I had done. This had all been for a good, important reason.

I settled in the backseat, barely breathing. Nobody said anything in the car going across town.

Nobody said anything when we got out and went into the house. Simon, wet and stained with mud, only thumped his tail at me from his pallet when I went inside. The kitchen smelled rich and spicy and Italian. Mom went straight to the stove and leaned over to check something in the oven.

"You'd better wash up for supper, Eliza," Dad said, opening the fridge to break out ice cubes for the pitcher.

They had gone from love to cold disapproval too fast for me to handle. I stood there a moment trying to make sense of it. They had been frantic with worry, according to Mr. Zloty. Maybe this was just shock and when it wore off, they would act normally again.

I tried to make myself obey Dad the way I always have when he tells me to do things. But I was too tired and shattered and miserable just to go away.

"Please," I begged.

Dad glanced at me and shook his head. "We'll have supper first, then we can talk."

"No," I said, louder than I ever speak up anywhere. "I don't want to go wash up. I want to tell you what happened."

My father turned on me quickly. He looked really tired, as if the past few hours had been years that had come out of nowhere to land on his face.

"We are more grateful than you'll ever know that we have you back safe and sound, Eliza, but we are also appalled. You see, while we were trying to find you, we learned what all has happened.

"We know that, in a brief few days you apparently forgot everything you've ever learned in your life. You sneaked out at night and broke into a house. You got into an ugly schoolyard fight. You deceived your mother about after-school plans. You dragged poor little Robin around in the rain until he nearly got pneumonia. Then, after you were called in by Mr. Heron for your well-deserved punishment, you ran away from school without being dismissed. Do you have any idea how much trouble you caused everyone? If Robin and Stephen hadn't convinced Mr. Zloty that you and Chris had probably gone out to that preserve to look for Ben Hardy, where do you think *you* would be now?"

I stared at him. I didn't want to think about that. I wanted Mom to pull me close again the way she had at the hospital and call me "Sweetie" and hug me tight. I wanted Dad to hug me again. I didn't need their disapproval. I didn't need them to act as if I had broken every rule in their book just for the fun of it.

All the anger and fear and frustration of the past few days boiled up inside me, blazing at the back of my throat the way vomit does. My voice sounded strange because of the burning.

"I knew Miss Dixon was in trouble," I said louder than I meant to. "Nobody was looking for her hard enough. Nobody was really thinking about where she would have gone. Somebody had to do *something*."

"Did it have to be you?" Dad asked, with even more sarcasm in his voice than he ordinarily uses during these awful "talks."

"Yes," I shouted, beginning to cry at the same time. And because it felt so good I kept shouting, "Yes, yes, yes" all the way upstairs and into my room where I slammed the door and locked it.

They both followed me up there but I ignored them. When they stood outside pounding on my door and ordering me to open up, I shoved a cassette into my stereo and turned the volume on high to drown them out. I could barely hear the doorbell over the beat of the music. The bell chimed a long time before they gave up and went downstairs to see who it was.

I jerked off my wet clothes and pulled on my terry cloth jumpsuit. The rain had started again, flooding down the glass of my windows and shining on the cars lined up in our street clear to the corner. I didn't know whose cars those were, and I didn't care. I didn't know who was downstairs talking to Mom and Dad, and I didn't care. I lay flat across my bed and felt a headache start to drum behind my eyes. What was one more hurt after all the others?

"It had to be me," I whispered over and over into the pillow. "There wasn't anybody else but me."

When the cassette ended, I got up to start it again. In that moment of silence I heard my name spoken quietly out in the hall.

"Eliza?" Miss Dixon's voice made my name a question. In that one word I could hear all the nice things that we both are — a little shy, not lively or outgoing, but knowing all the time what we believe in and want to say.

I stood a long moment before unlocking the door. She didn't move but just stood smiling at me before holding out her arms. She didn't pat me or anything. She just held me and talked in a low and steady voice about how grateful she was that I had cared. "Parents get mad when they're worried, just the way we do," she told me. "They're over that now, and I think your mother is crying."

I stood very still. Mom is into self-control, not crying.

"You might want to come down and let Mrs. Hardy apologize, too," she said softly. "We could go together."

She hadn't told me that Stephen and Mr. Zloty were there, too, along with Mr. Heron and Robin grinning from his regular stool over by the TV set. I would have known Dr. Cobb the physicist, even if he hadn't been sitting right next to Chris. He had whitish, thick hair combed too close over his face just like Chris's. Mom wasn't crying, but I could tell she had been from her mascara streaks.

Mr. Heron had especially asked to talk to me. I had never seen him apologize before, but he was really rather graceful about it. "I should have known," he said at the last. "We have always been able to depend on Eliza to do what needed to be done — in her own quiet way, of course."

I tried not to look at Mom but I couldn't help it. She had the sides of her mouth pulled down like a mouse, too, and was beginning to cry as she reached for me.

14
Final Developments

Everybody talked at once. For a while it looked as if nobody was ever going to go home. But it was almost worth being so awfully tired to learn some of the things I did that night.

It turned out that Miss Dixon was only a little bit dehydrated. She promised to come back to school Friday afternoon for the class Halloween party.

Benjamin Hardy's mother tried but couldn't really choke out an apology for the way she had talked to me. She did manage to thank me for going back out to look for her "poor child," who had to have seven stitches put in his leg where the guard dog had grabbed him and wrestled him down. And a tetanus shot, too.

Mr. Zloty and the other investigators had good clear pictures both of the thieves and the license on their station wagon. They also had fingerprints from the boxes of chemicals that the men had left in the shanty when they made their escape. All those pictures had been behind the door of that locked darkroom in the basement of Miss Dixon's house the whole time.

I tried to grab a chance to tell everybody that things had only turned out so well because Chris had been so down-to-earth smart. After all, he had figured out where I was going and had told Stephen and Robin before he left to come help me. I thought Chris was going to strangle me.

"Lay off, Eliza," he begged in a fierce whisper. "Let's not wimp out on each other. I won't give you away if you won't rat on me."

This kind of talk from the lad with the impossible vocabulary and the hang-up with science?

"I don't understand," I told him. "It's only fair for you to get the credit."

He shook his head solemnly. "First, it was you all the way. Stephen and Robin and I only backed you up. As for either one of us getting credit for what happened, forget it! Do you want to be branded as a hero? Come on now, be honest, was that fun?"

I stared at him in horror. "FUN! This has been the most awful, dreadful week of my whole entire life."

He nodded, grinning. "See? Now this alien sky-watch I fool around with really *is* fun! A lot of us guys twist our telescopes around and send frantic messages back and forth on our modems and read the bulletins that come out of NASA. As long as everybody sees me as a space cadet, I won't have to drag any smelly Ben Hardys out of muddy holes and risk being eaten alive by snakes and guard dogs. As long as people still think of you as a nice quiet little person who specializes in minding her own business, you can do your own thing without anybody butting in. Tell me that's not a good deal!"

It took me a minute but I finally grinned. He was right. I had been proud of myself being able to do what I thought needed to be done to find Miss Dixon. But hated to think that I would have to show that side of myself all the time. I liked being the way I'd always been, but knowing that I could act on my convictions if I needed to.

"Only one more thing," he said, his pale eyes shining. "If the chips *are* ever down again, don't hesitate to call on me, okay?"

I saw Stephen and Robin grinning over at us and thought about the other kids in our class. Mostly I thought about Perky. After all, she's my second best friend and I had done nothing but be cross at her for days!

Robin saw my look and leaned close. "What's the matter, Eliza?" he asked.

"Perky," I said. "She's going to be furious at me for not letting her know what was going on."

Chris laughed. "She had her chance to solve this

mystery along with the rest of us. Anyway, she's probably at home right now trying to make up some bad jokes about it."

When everyone finally left, I dropped into bed. I thought I would fall asleep before I hit the pillow but I didn't. I kept hearing the soft murmur of Mom and Dad's voices coming from their room down the hall.

I wondered if they were giving each other one of those talks. Maybe they were even worrying about how to deal with their Eliza-turned-monster overnight.

I wriggled deeper under the covers. My parents didn't need to worry. I liked the way it had ended, knowing I could perform under pressure, but that didn't mean I was going to make a habit of it.

I thought at first I was going to miss the class Halloween party. When Mom saw my cuts and bruises, she took me in for a tetanus shot and then out to buy jeans to replace the ones I had ruined in the preserve. Afterward, she even took me for lunch and a peanut buster parfait, in spite of the way our dentist is always lecturing us both about my eating sweets.

When I got to our classroom that Friday afternoon, I looked up at the front of the room and let out a yowl. It couldn't be happening. I couldn't stand it.

A single piece of computer paper stretched as long and as high as the blackboard. All the kids had signed their names along the edges but WELCOME BACK, MISS SUPERMOUSE was spelled down the middle in giant black letters. Underneath, in smaller letters, was written: AND ELIZA PHARIS, SUPER SLEUTH.

The mouse part was what almost made me take after those kids. Nobody wanted to be called "Mouse" or "mousy" even if it stood for somebody with that quiet kind of strength Miss Dixon has. I couldn't make a scene because Mr. Heron and Miss Dixon came in right behind me. Mr. Heron stared at the sign with his mouth open, but Miss Dixon clapped both hands and laughed right out loud.

"Oh, class. That's wonderful," she cried. "I've been called 'Supermouse' by my three brothers since I was about ten. Before that, they had started calling me just 'Mouse' because I was so much smaller than they were. They changed it to 'Supermouse' when they discovered I wasn't afraid to stand up to them. Having my old nickname back *really* makes me feel at home with you kids."

For once, Benjamin Hardy didn't jump up and claim the credit. Instead, he just grinned and ducked his head and a lot of the kids even looked over at him and smiled.

About the Author

MARY FRANCIS SHURA is the author of sixty-nine books, including *The Josie Gambit*, an ALA Notable; *The Search for Grissi*, recipient of a Carl Sandburg Literary Arts Award for Children's Literature; and *Chester* and *Eleanor*, IRA-CBC Joint Committee Children's Choices.

Ms. Shura wrote several other novels including *Kate's Book*, *Kate's House*, *Jessica*, and *The Mystery at Wolf River*.